Unintentionally Connected

Thomas Valentine

Copyright © 2015 Thomas Valentine
All rights reserved
First Edition

PAGE PUBLISHING, INC.
New York, NY

First originally published by Page Publishing, Inc. 2015

ISBN 978-1-68213-546-4 (pbk)
ISBN 978-1-68213-547-1 (digital)

Printed in the United States of America

I would like to dedicate my first published book to my parents Thomas E. Valentine Sr. (deceased) and my mother Geraldine Valentine and my wife Geisha.

Part I

It's early August in the year 1982, right around 4:00 p.m. The Valdosta heat is really getting to Bruce Wilson. It's superhot that day. There was not a cloud in the sky. Bruce has had that construction job for approximately seven months now. And even though he was putting in close to sixty hours a week, it was still rough due to the fact that he was not really making top pay, and the child support from a previous relationship was really draining his weekly pay. Bruce has another son, Martell, now about five years old, who lived in Ohio. Bruce's rent was behind along with his credit card bills. Bruce and his wife Leatha lived on the south side of Valdosta, on a dirt road. The street was called Twitty Lane.

Bruce hears the 4:30 p.m. whistle, signifying that it was finally time to get off of that tractor and run to the locker room to get changed pick his check up and go home. Bruce passed his coworkers as they all planned their weekly guys' night out at the local club for beer, pool, and guy talk. Bruce, not really interested, passed on all the offers, so he can leave and get to the store to take groceries home because Leatha had been complaining about needing milk, salt, and other items, so she could cook for dinner. She also fussed about not having any toilet paper at the house, and she bugged him to death about it. She kept calling him at the job about getting to the store as quickly as possible.

Bruce entered into the boss's office, grabbed his check, proceeded out the office door and headed to his truck. He opened his check to find $325 weekly pay. His truck was sort of beat up. It's an old blue Ford extended-cab pickup. Bruce and Leatha didn't really have a lot of money. They had two vehicles; one was an old Oldsmobile, which happened to be sitting on bricks in the yard. It needed a motor and a battery.

Bruce put his check in his wallet and headed off to the store, where he sometimes cashed his checks. He and Leatha did have a bank account, but it was overdrawn, and he couldn't afford paying the penalty, so he cashed his checked at the store. He was able pick up his items and proceed to the truck.

Bruce got home with the groceries and the leftover money from his check. He was greeted at the door by Leatha, who gave him a big kiss. She couldn't really hug him tight because her stomach was so big by her being pregnant. They both put the groceries up, and Leatha started her dinner while Bruce went to take the dog out and grab the mail.

While gathering the mail, he noticed that the bills were piling up, and it was so frustrating to him that he just didn't have enough to pay everything off. He went on down the road with Roscoe, the German shepherd, who was just his big, loving baby. They would go walking every evening, and Bruce would sing while walking Roscoe. Bruce happened to be a very talented and gifted pianist/ singer in which he played for his church there in Valdosta. They walked for thirty minutes and returned home to eat.

After dinner, Bruce cleaned up the dishes and the kitchen because Leatha had to lay down because her belly started hurting, and being pregnant, she was in pain from the baby moving around and kicking.

Finally, all the dishes were put up, and the kitchen was clean. Bruce sat at his old upright piano that the church let him have after they had purchased a new one. They allowed him to have it, so he could practice on it at home at his leisure. He often wrote songs for his church choir on this old upright piano. So he started to play a song he learned called "Just Call His Name." Leatha just loved hearing her husband play and sing. After playing for about an hour, it was time for bed. He hit the shower and headed toward the bedroom. Roscoe was right behind him.

Early Saturday morning arrived, and again, it looked as though it was going to be a hot day in Valdosta. The birds were chirping, and one could smell that early-morning country scent. Leatha was up in the bathroom, sick again. Bruce was still lying there on his side of the bed, and Roscoe wanted to go out. Leatha made it back to the bed, and she snuggled next to Bruce. She said to him, "Honey, are we gonna be able to afford having a family? Will we be able to make it?" Bruce reassured her that everything will be okay, and that he would do whatever he had to to protect and raise his family. Leatha had family in Miami, whom she had to, on several occasions, ask for financial help. All of Leatha's family was in Miami. She came to Valdosta to attend Valdosta State on an academic scholarship, which she did for two years. She had an aunt, Dorena, with whom she lived with while attending school. Aunt Dorena just happened to be a member of Morning Star Baptist Church like Bruce. That was how she met Bruce. They dated while she was in college for several months and fell in love. Dorena suddenly became gravely ill, and she eventually passed from her sickness. Leatha moved back on campus for a while, but things just weren't working out for her financially. Leatha dropped out of college after two years, and she and Bruce moved in together. They got married and have been married for a little over two years.

Bruce remembered that there was a Saturday football game at the high school, so he wanted to go, but he couldn't afford it because money was really tight even for a football game. Valdosta High had the best high school football team in the state. Bruce had played high school football there at Valdosta years prior.

While lying there, Leatha jumped up screaming, and she started breathing heavily. She started bleeding from her womb. Immediately, Bruce rushed her to the hospital.

After being seen by the doctor, he told Bruce that everything was going to be okay, but they wanted to keep her for observation for the night. So Bruce's plans for possibly going to that game were shot. He didn't care; he just wanted his wife and baby well. He stayed at with Leatha at the hospital the whole day, only leaving to go back and take Roscoe for a walk, and then it was back to the hospital. She was discharged the next day, and the Wilson family headed home.

It was early Sunday morning. It had been a couple months since Leatha's discharge from the hospital. Everything had been going fine. Bruce was still putting in the hours at the job and taking care of Leatha. He had just finished walking Roscoe. Leatha was all ready for church, but she's complaining about not wearing her heels because of her pregnancy. She had to settle for her flip-flops. Leatha was very petite and loved wearing her stiletto heels.

While sitting in the third row of the church, Leatha was really getting into the choir's song and Bruce was up at the organ, playing his heart out. Suddenly, Leatha felt a sharp pain in her belly. The pain got more intense as the songs from the choir went on. Leatha then collapsed on the pew. Bruce saw this and immediately stopped playing the organ and rant to her aide. Several of the church ladies join in and came to her aide.

They got her in the car, and Bruce raced off to the hospital. A few of the members were following behind them to the hospital.

They finally got her to the ER, and the hospital staff immediately got her in the back to labor and delivery. Several of the members from the church had now arrived to the hospital to support Bruce and Leatha. Bruce didn't have the strength to go into the delivery room, so he waited in the waiting room with some of the church members. After about an hour, the doctor came out to inform Bruce that he was now the father of a healthy baby girl. Bruce was so happy, and the church members were celebrating with him. Suddenly, the nurse ran from the back and grabbed the doctor and said he needed to get back to the labor and delivery room immediately. The doctor rushed back into the labor and delivery room. Now Bruce was starting to get worried.

Thirty minutes had passed, and still there was no other information from the hospital staff. The members of the church were all getting a little agitated in the waiting room. All of a sudden, the doctor came out to talk to Bruce. The doctor happily informed him that not only were Leatha and the baby fine, but that there was another. It was a little boy. The little baby boy was fine, and they didn't expect a twin, but the doctor said that the baby boy was very little and that he was never noticed by any of the prenatal tests that were administered.

The church members that were in the waiting room cheered but, shortly thereafter, had to leave because the hospital staff complained of the noise level.

Bruce finally got back into the recovery room to see his lovely wife and his little girl, but the baby boy was in the incubator, being tended to by the nursing staff.

Bruce and Leatha didn't expect twins, and now they had to come up with some names. They chose Misty for the little girl and Mitchell for the little boy.

The doctors came into the room to talk with the couple about their new additions to the family. The doctor explained that the twins were fraternal. Meaning they were not going to look alike, and that Mitchell may need more extensive medical care, him being so little. He may also suffer from some respiratory complications as he grows up. The babies got their little footprints and their pictures done, and they're back in the room.

Two days had gone by since the birth of the twins, and now it's time to go home. The doctors were allowing Mitchell to go home as well. His progress was really good after those couple of days in the hospital. His lungs strengthened up enough to go home, but the pediatrician wanted to see him in two weeks for a further examination.

Bruce had been working during the daytime hours, and he would come to the hospital in the evenings to spend with his family. He had really been doing everything one could ask of a husband.

While his family was in the hospital, he was also preparing the newborns' bedroom at their home.

It's time to go, and Leatha was getting the babies, Misty and Mitchell, ready to go home, and Bruce had gone to the parking lot to get the truck. While doing so, Leatha noticed how feisty Misty was and thinking to herself that two little babies were going to be a true handful. She said a quick little prayer thanking God for her two little blessings. Mrs. Willie Mae Tizzy stopped in for a quick second. She's the elder's wife of the church, who just wanted to get a sneak peak of the kids. She had her camera with her, and she wanted to get some pictures of the beautiful little babies. She took several shots as Leatha was getting the babies dressed, and she noticed the dark footprint-shaped birthmark on the babies' backs that were both in the same place. The footprint-shaped marks were on the lower right back. Mrs. Tizzy thought it was so cute. So she took more pictures, and she told Leatha that she would get copies to her and Bruce real soon. So she said good-bye because she was off to do more elder wives' duties, in other words, visiting the sick.

The nurse finally showed up with the wheelchair, and Leatha and her two new blessings were in her arms, being rolled down to the truck where an anxious Bruce was waiting with the door opened. He had two new car seats in the backseat of his truck that a family member had bought as a present to the family. The babies were placed in the car, and Leatha got in her spot in the front, and Bruce drove off into the Valdosta sun. He's so excited that his new family was finally going home. All of his financial worries were behind him for the moment.

It has now been around three months since the babies have been in this world. They were really doing well and now sleeping all night. Bruce was still putting in several hours at his job. Since the birth of his children, the boss at the construction had given him a small raise, but not anything to jump for joy about. Even Roscoe had taken to the kids. He sat by the cribs and guarded them all night, and Bruce just loved this.

UNINTENTIONALLY CONNECTED

Lately, Bruce has noticed how Leatha had really been sort of rude to him. She was starting to complain about money, money, money. She had been complaining about how he didn't spend enough time at home and that he should find another job that paid more money and had less hours. She also had been complaining about Bruce's family not stepping in to help like they should. He ignored it when she started to yell at him for reasons that were not even worth a fight. One night at the house, it got so bad that he actually left and went to the pool hall to meet some of his coworkers. Leatha had thrown a shoe at him because he forgot to take the trash out one night, and it started to stink up the house. She also cursed him heavily because one night he didn't hear little Mitchell crying because he needed to be changed. She called some of her family members in Miami and told them that Bruce allowed all their bills to be paid late because he was mismanaging all the money. Bruce was working double shifts, and he was just really tired when he got home. So when he lay down, he was totally out for the count. He was exhausted. There were nights were he didn't even have the energy to walk Roscoe.

One late morning while at work, Bruce called the family physician and told him what was going on at the house. He explained to the doctor that Leatha had been just yelling at him and throwing things at him. He told the doctor that everything that he was doing for the family just wasn't good enough for her and that she put him down in every situation he could think of, even to the point of rejecting his intimate advances and calling him names in front of the babies and sometimes family. Bruce told the doctor that it was even affecting his piano playing at the church. He can't concentrate.

The doctor let Bruce vent for a while on the phone. He felt that Bruce needed to vent. The doctor came back and explained that Leatha was experiencing postpartum depression, and that her emotions were up and down. The doctor also told him to just have patience and continue to do the right things and just continue to be there for that beautiful family that God had blessed him with. Bruce didn't really understand at that moment what postpartum was, but he told the doctor that he would do his best to ignore her comments and just continue trying to be that good father and husband.

Bruce had really good parents. His father was also in construction, and his mother was a bank teller. They were strong church people who had strong beliefs in the importance of the family structure. They raised Bruce to be a good family man. Bruce was an only child, and now both parents are deceased. Leatha, on the other hand, didn't have both parents in the household. Her father left her mother while Leatha was only seven. She never really had that family structure like Bruce did.

It was Sunday, and Bruce was up early, walking his buddy Roscoe while singing a song he was going to sing at church in a few hours. It was good to get out in the early morning Valdosta air. He felt as though he needed that alone time due to the fact that the night before, Leatha once again cussed him out so bad for not having enough money to buy new furniture for the house, and she told him that he was not a man and that he needed a new job. As these thoughts grew heavily on his mind he just sang louder, and it appeared that even Roscoe was loving it as well.

Bruce returned to the house to find that the babies were still sleeping, and Leatha was still in the bed. She lay there crying her heart out, and she explained to Bruce that she was sorry for how she had been treating him the last few months. She also said that she loved him, and she didn't know what was wrong with her. She knew she missed her family in Miami, and she hadn't seen them in months. She told him that the doctor had wanted to see her in a week or so to examine her and that the babies had their appointments in a week as well. Bruce lay next to her and held her. She kissed him on the forehead and told him that she wasn't going to church that morning because she didn't feel like it and that he could take Misty with him. Mitchell was going to stay at home with her. Misty took well with Bruce. She would immediately stop crying whenever Bruce picked her up, but as for Mitchell, he was totally turning into a mama's boy. He could only sleep when she was around or with his sister. Even when in church, Mitchell didn't like when any of the men held him, but when those sisters got ahold of him, he was either smiling or sleeping.

Bruce insisted that he stay at home that morning to be with his family, but Leatha insisted that he go on to church because he was playing the piano and singing that morning. Misty will go with Daddy, said Leatha. She knew that the sisters of the church will occupy Misty while Bruce was doing his thing on the organ. As a matter of fact, even when Leatha was at church, she rarely held the twins because everyone wanted to hold them.

So Bruce took his shower and he got a bite to eat and also fed the babies as Roscoe looked on. He finally got dressed, and he prepared the baby bag for Misty, since she would be accompanying him that morning. As Bruce takes the baby bag to the car he notices that Leatha doesn't look normal. He could tell that something was really bothering her. He remembered what the doctor had said to him on the phone that she might be suffering from postpartum syndrome. So he came back into the house, and he kissed Mitch on the forehead, and he reached for Misty. As he grabbed her, he turned around and he kissed Leatha on the forehead and then on the lips. He said, "I love you, honey, and please don't worry about anything." She told him that she loved him too and that she'll be okay when they got back from morning worship services. She hugged and kissed Bruce and little Misty one more time before turning around to get Mitch and head back to the bedroom to lie down. Bruce walked out the door with Misty in his arms, and they're off to church.

While at church, little Misty was passed around from arm to arm along with her diaper bag. Bruce got up to the organ, and the choir stood up. He started to play, and the choir started to sing. Bruce started to sing as well, and he started to adlib like never before. The spirit was really in him because he was singing well beyond his range. It was like his emotions were pouring out and being portrayed in his singing. You could hear the abundance of joy and happiness all together coming out of his voice. The church was alive and rocking.

Even little Misty, who was asleep in one of the deacon wives' arms woke up when she heard her daddy singing his heart out in the front.

At home, Leatha was getting up to see about Mitchell, who was crying loudly. He needed to be changed, and it was almost his feeding time anyway. Leatha just started crying because she was really tired, and she missed her family dearly. Sometimes she just starts crying out of the blue for no apparent reason, and she didn't understand why. It was getting more frequent lately.

Bruce and Misty returned home. On the way, Bruce stopped and picked up a bucket of chicken for a nice Sunday dinner with his family. He knew that Leatha was not feeling up to cooking. He opened the door, holding the baby and the bucket of chicken, and Leatha was standing in the hallway, holding Mitch. Leatha had no expression of joy whatsoever on her face. Before, she would have greeted Bruce at the door with a kiss or would be by his side. Now that the babies were born, her emotions were running crazy to the point she didn't even realize that about herself. She did prepare some paper plates and she grabbed some iced tea from in the refrigerator. She also prepared the babies' bottles and put both kids in their little seats. It was actually nap time for them anyway.

They sat down to eat in front of the television, and Leatha just started to cry. She told Bruce that she missed her family and that she wanted to go and see them in Miami. Bruce said, "Whatever you want, honey, to make you feel better." He told her that he just wanted the old Leatha back. She replied, "Honey, I'm trying, but I need to see my family."

Bruce told her that he would see about getting her a bus ticket that weekend for Miami. He had to wait for his check on Friday. That was not good enough for Leatha, but it had to do for now. She was so impatient that she wanted her ticket in hand that instant.

So things were the same throughout the week in the Wilson household. Leatha was still having crying spells and arguing with Bruce about very minor things. When Friday finally arrived, Bruce had purchased her ticket from the bus station on his lunch hour. He called Leatha at home and told her the news, and she's happy. She would be leaving for Miami next Wednesday evening. Now, she's thinking of who could help Bruce with the babies while she was gone. There was no way she could take both on the bus with her, and neither could she leave both with Bruce because of his work schedule. She decided that she would take Mitch with her because he needed a little more attention since he was not as healthy as Misty. Mitch still was much smaller, and he cried more. Leatha got on the phone and asked Bruce's cousin Mary if she could help Bruce watched after little Misty while she was gone. She figured that Mary could help since she was retired and had nothing but time on her hands. Mary replied yes, and now her plans were coming to life.

Meanwhile, Steve Bennett, a very successful, high-profile thirty-seven-year-old attorney who lived in Macon, Georgia, just took his wife Jean a housewife to the fertility clinic at the hospital in Macon, Georgia. The doctor called back Steve and Jean for the results of a test that she had two weeks ago. Steve and Jean had been trying to become pregnant for several years now and had not been successful. They hadn't had any prior children, and Jean was desperate to have a child. The doctor informed them that once again her tests were coming up negative for pregnancy. Steve has had a test on himself as well to determine if his sperm count was normal. His were fine, but her tests all showed that, for some reason, she had a problem with her ovaries.

When the doctor gave her the disappointing news, Jean just started crying and grabbing at Steve with force. Jean was very soft spoken. Steve, on the other hand, was very outgoing, loud at times, and aggressive. He had to be because of his very high profile job as an attorney and his political status there in Macon. The doctor offered another suggestion to them which might be very expensive, but it didn't matter to Steve because he was basically a millionaire. Steve had been earning a six-figure salary for about ten years now. The doctor told them that they could have a surrogate mother carry their child and/or they could just adopt. Steve looked at the doctor while holding his wife and told him that they would go home and think about it and that he would get back to him within a few weeks.

Leaving the doctor's office, Jean still remained within her husband's arms. They walked to the black BMW holding each other, and Jean was still crying her eyes out. She was so disappointed and hurt. Steve put her in the car, and he went around to get in, and they left the parking lot.

They arrived at the mansion of a house that they own, and their maid of five years, Hazel, came out to the car as it turned in the driveway. Hazel opened the door to help Jean get out, and Jean just grabbed Hazel really tight and started crying even harder. Hazel tried to console her as she walked her through the door. Hazel sat her on the couch, and she ran into the kitchen to retrieve some sedatives for Jean, so she could relax and take a nap. Steve was getting some things out of the car, and he also came in to see about his wife. Hazel went and fixed him his martini, and Steve thanked her. The Bennetts had an excellent relationship with Hazel. She practically was a part of the family. When Steve and Jean would take exotic trips, Hazel often tagged along with them.

The phone in Steve's office downstairs rang, so he ran to the office to answer it. He had been waiting for an important phone call from the firm. Instead, it was a good friend, Gary, who he went out and had drinks with and drove to Atlanta to go to some of the Falcon's and Brave's games. Steve told Gary what had happened at the doctor's office and how bad of a shape Jean was in. Gary told him, "Man, y'all drive down to the Keys and spend time together away from everyone." Steve told him that that was a very good idea and that he would do just that. Steve got off the phone and ran back into the living room where Jean was on the couch, but she now was totally asleep. The sedative had finally knocked her out. Hazel stood there and watched over her.

Steve explained to Hazel that he would be taking Jean to the Keys for a few weeks to take her mind off things, and that they would be leaving on Wednesday. It was a Monday. Hazel told him that she would have everything ready by then. Steve headed upstairs to lie down himself.

Later that evening, Jean woke up from a lengthy nap to find that Hazel had prepared a big Southern home-cooked meal for the family. Steve himself still slept upstairs. Hazel explained to Jean that Steve had something to tell her something. So Jean ran upstairs to find Steve lying across the bed, and she snuggled up to him, massaging his forehead. He cracked one of his eyes open, and she kissed him on the forehead and told him that she was sorry for how she reacted earlier that day in the doctor's office. Steve jumped up and told her that she had nothing to be sorry for, and that he understood how she felt because he wanted a child too. Jean told him that that may be God's plan. "So we just have to try and move on."

Steve, in his low voice, said, "I have a surprise," and Jean excitedly asked, "What? What is it, honey?" Steve told her the news that they would be driving down to Key West on Wednesday to a condo where they will be spending a few weeks to get away and to get their minds off of everything that was going on. Jean hugged Steve really tight and gave him a very deep kiss. She was really excited about the trip.

The trip was something different to them because they always took cruises, and they had been to all the islands. They've been overseas plenty of times, but this time, they were gonna stay close to home.

They both went downstairs to that wonderful dinner Hazel had prepared. Jean was excited. She only had two days to pack. Steve had to take care of a couple of things at work, but he needed that trip too.

It's now Wednesday morning, and Steve was getting ready to go into the office. He had to take care of some clients' paperwork before they could get on the road for Key West. Jean and Hazel were in the kitchen having coffee and talking about the trip. Jean already had her clothes packed, and she's excited. So Steve grabbed his donut and his coffee mug Hazel always prepared for him in the morning. He then kissed Jean and waves good-bye to Hazel, and he was off to work.

On the way to work, Steve was thinking to himself that that was going to be a good trip, and that they were going to have a wonderful time. He stopped and got the car a good wash then he was in the office, behind his desk.

On Tuesday evening, Leatha thought in her mind that she needed to give Bruce the best loving he had ever had before she left. She knew in her mind that she had been treating him really bad lately, and she couldn't explain why her emotions were going the way they were. She called up Bruce's aunt to see if she could watch the babies that night for her. So Bruce's aunt drove over, and she picked up the twins, but she only had one car seat, so she picked up Misty first and drove to her home to her husband and then she returned to get Mitch and then she left. Valdosta is a small city, so it was basically very short two trips. Leatha also took Roscoe out for his walk, and they quickly returned.

Leatha knew that Bruce would be getting home soon, so she quickly prepared a quick little petite dinner, and then she put on her high heels and her thigh-high stockings. She knew that Bruce had a fetish about her in stilettos, so she wanted to blow his mind before she left for Miami even though she was only going to be there for a few days.

That night, Bruce drove into the driveway. He got out, and he climbed up the porch, and before he could get his key out, Leatha opened the door and pulled him in. Bruce looked at her in amazement, and he was getting very excited. She pulled him into the bathroom where there was a hot bubble bath waiting with candles around the tub. He immediately asked, "Where are the kids?" She replied, "They're taken care of."

Bruce took his bath, and when he got out of the tub, he found Leatha at the dinner table with his plate. Bruce ate his food, and they both had a glass of red wine. She then jumped onto Bruce, kissing and caressing him. Bruce picked her up and they went into the bedroom, and next thing was her heels were in the air. It had been a very long time since they had been intimate, and they were making up for lost time. They made love throughout the night and into the early Wednesday morning hours.

Bruce eventually called his boss and took a sick day from work. He was determined to spend the day with his lovely wife and his babies.

At 6:00 p.m. on Wednesday, Leatha had hers and Mitch's bag packed; she also had a baby carrier for Mitch that someone gave them at the baby shower. Bruce was holding Misty, and they both were watching Leatha get all this stuff together.

Bruce takes all of the bags to the car and they put the twins into the car seats and they're off to the bus station.

They finally arrived at the bus station. Then it was actually time for them to board, so Bruce, holding Mitch, and Leatha, holding Misty, did a group hug. Bruce looked as though he wanted to tear up because they've never been separated since they have been together. Bruce kissed Mitch on his cheek, and Mitch sort of laughed. Then Leatha kissed Misty. Leatha and Bruce both kissed, then Leatha and Mitch boarded the bus. She was going to call just as soon as she and Mitch arrived at Miami. Bruce waved and he watched them take their seats, and then the bus pulled off into the evening. Bruce and Misty then got back into the truck, and they headed for the house. Misty looked as though she misses her mommy and brother already.

Steve and Jean had already been on the road headed South on I-75. Steve had the jazz playing, and Jean was just sitting back in her seat, excited. Steve knew that it would be a very long drive, so he had all the good jazz and old school CDs ready.

On the bus, Leatha was playing with Mitch's feet and making him laugh. She still had him strapped in his baby carrier. The two ladies in the seats across the aisle kept making faces at Mitch, making him laugh. Everything is going smoothly, Leatha thought. She was worried that Mitch would be acting up because it was his first long trip, and he was still very little.

All of a sudden, a truck from the northbound side of I-75 crossed the median and entered into oncoming traffic. Everyone heard the bus driver scream. The bus driver tried to swerve out of the way. Leatha covered Mitch as best as she could. Everyone was screaming at the top of their lungs. The truck hit the bus broadside and sent the bus tumbling off the road and into a creek. Then there was an explosion. A fire ball went into the dusk of the night.

It just so happened that Steve and Jean saw that terrible accident. They were approximately two hundred yards away. Steve drove as close as he could to the scene of the accident to see if he could help. He stopped the BMW and jumped out. He ran down the embankment, and fire was everywhere. The bus was lying on its side. He saw several bodies that had been thrown from the bus onto the grass, some into the creek. He didn't see any signs of life. Suddenly, he heard the cries of a baby. He followed the sounds to find a little baby still in the carrier with a small amount of blood around the baby's foot. He grabbed the handle of the baby carrier and brushed all the glass off and ran to the car. He left the baby blanket behind. It had glass and blood all over it. Jean was in the car, scared to death. She saw Steve returning to the car, holding something. She opened her door. Steve yelled, "Get back in the car, honey! We gotta go." He can't believe no authorities or EMS services had arrived yet. He then opened his door, and he put the baby in the car and onto Jean's lap. The baby was just crying and screaming. Steve looked into Jean's face and said, "Baby, we gotta go." They stared at each other intently for a bit. Both were thinking the same thing, What do we do? Jean took the little baby out of the seat, and she checked to make sure medical attention was not needed. It appeared that the seat protected the little baby from any injury. Steve quickly drove off, and he crossed the median and drove back, northbound on I-75 because I-75 southbound was covered in debris and bodies. He looked at Jean and said, "Honey, we gotta go. We gotta go back home."

She totally understood, and they proceeded northbound toward Macon. They stopped and bought diapers and formula for the baby, who had since calmed down a little. Steve had to buy a bottle and everything. For a moment, the two forgot that the little baby belonged to someone else. Jean changed the baby, and then she found that the baby was a little boy. They proceeded back to Macon. The car was totally quiet on the way back; the little baby was asleep. The little one had been through so much, and his little body was probably worn out. He had a new bottle, and he was asleep in the arms of Jean as Steve drove.

Back at the scene, the police and emergency medical services had finally arrived. The news reporters from Florida and also Georgia were gathering. The accident took place right inside of the Florida state line. Helicopters were everywhere. CNN's reporters just happened to be close by, covering a story, so they showed up at the scene as well. The police combed the area as the fire department continued to put out the fires that were everywhere. The big semitruck was totally engulfed in flames, and there were no signs of life in the truck. It appeared that a body inside the cab was burning to a black crisp. The bus had flipped more than once, and it rolled off the side of the embankment. The top of the bus was crushed as part of it was in the water. All of the glass in the bus was busted out. The driver of the bus lay lifeless with the bus resting on his lower torso. The bus, as it rolled off the side of the road, crushed two cars. All of the occupants of the cars were dead. They were crushed to death. The police chief in charge finally talked with a reporter from CNN and the local news station and started to explain the situation that there was a very horrible crash that took place on I-75 southbound involving a crowded bus, a semitruck, and two small compact cars. The chief said it didn't appear that there were any signs of life, but that they were still investigating the scene. It was dark, but all the lights from the helicopters and lights from all the media made it look so bright. All of I-75 southbound was shut down throughout the night.

Early Thursday morning, Bruce was getting Misty ready to go over his aunt's house. He's already taken Roscoe on his walk. He got his lunch, and he and Misty headed out of the door.

At lunchtime, Bruce went to the breakroom to have his lunch. Before he went into the room, he stopped at the phone in one of the offices to call and check on Misty. His aunt assured him that she's fine and that she was just about to have her bottle.

Bruce entered the breakroom where everyone was gathered around the television. Bruce sat at the table and opened his lunchbox. He focused on the TV and heard the reported say, "This is the worst crash in Florida history." It grabbed Bruce's attention. So Bruce got up from the table, and he approached the TV to see a crane behind the reporter pulling a bus upright. Bruce immediately told everyone to shut up, so he could hear, since there was so much chatter going on. Then the reporter interviewed a crash investigator, and he started to explain how the accident happened and when it happened. Bruce screamed to the top of his lungs, "My family! Please, God, not my family! Noooooo!"

He ran to the boss's office and told him he had to go. He explained that his wife may have been in that horrible accident. The boss immediately told Bruce to go and that if he needed anything, to let him know. One of Bruce's coworkers gave him some money, and he told him that he was in his prayers. He said, "Go, and take care of your family."

Bruce thanked him, and he ran to the truck. He took off to his aunt's house where little Misty was sleeping, and he explained that Leatha and Mitch were in a horrible accident. He asked if she could watch over Misty while he was gone, and he gave her the house key because she would have to let Roscoe out and feed him. His aunt was ecstatic. She said, "Go, hon. We got this," referring to taking care of Misty and Roscoe.

Bruce took off for southbound section of I-75, and he really didn't know where he was headed, but he knew he had to get there. He knew this happened on the southbound lane of I-75 somewhere, not really far away. It just so happened that his truck did have a full tank of gas. After driving for over an hour, Bruce came into the area where the accident happened. They still had the barricades blocking the left lane. Bruce pulled off the expressway onto the service drive, and he asked one of the investigators that his wife was possibly on that bus. The investigator humbly informed him that no one survived the accident, and that he needed to go to the local morgue to identify any family member. The investigator gave him the address as to where to go.

Bruce cried like a baby. He actually threw up while on the way to his truck. He couldn't grasp the fact that his wife and his son were dead.

He arrived at the county morgue. It was only twenty minutes away from the scene. He walked in and had to give all of his information and the information of the loved ones that were possibly lost. He gave the info about Leatha and then he gave the info about little Mitchell. The coroner said, "We possibly have your wife, but there was no infant found."

Bruce said, "How can that be? He was with my wife!"

The coroner said that there was no evidence that they had an infant or its remains located there at the morgue. Bruce just dropped his head. The coroner took Bruce back to the viewing area, but there were so many he had to look at to identify. He saw the first five bodies and neither were his wife and then the coroner rolled out another gurney and he pulls back the zipper on the body bag and it contained the body of his wife Leatha. She was badly burned and her head was crushed. Bruce almost fainted, and with a sigh, he told the coroner that it was his wife. Oh, he cried so bad. Behind him, more people started to flow in to claim their loved ones. There was still no sign of Mitchell. He just thought the worse since he saw what had happened to his wife. Shortly after making the necessary arrangements to have her body shipped back to Valdosta, he decided to go to the police station where the investigators were. He arrived there in tears and all of his energy was drained. He walked in an asked to talk to the investigators on this case. He met with Captain Sully, who explained that there was no evidence of an infant at the scene of the accident. He said that they have gathered all the evidence from the scene, and it's was maintained as a holding area so that they could finish working on their investigation. Bruce explained that his little son was with his wife on that bus. The captain said that he will pay special attention to any evidence that suggested that there was an infant. He also stated that he would put out a search and rescue team. He got all Bruce's information and told him to go home and get himself together and just let time heal itself. Bruce left to return home. That was the longest drive Bruce had ever done. He had to pass the scene of the accident on the way home. He just looked over at the burn marks in the expressway. He was headed northbound, and he was looking on the southbound side. He just cried all the way back home.

 He reached his house and just sat in the car, looking at the house. All he knew at that point was that he would have to be there for little Misty and raise her alone. He collapsed on the steering wheel of the truck in exhaustion, and he would remain there throughout the night.

Meanwhile, the Bennett's had since arrived at their home, and Hazel was in shock because she saw this cute little boy in Jean's arms. She wasn't expecting them back for at least a week or so. Of course, she questioned, "Whose baby?"

They all went to the big dinner table to talk. Steve said that the little baby's mother and/or father were probably dead from the accident. Steve said that they probably thought that the little guy was dead as well. Hazel informed them that she had seen the news of that accident, and that it looked to be very horrible and gruesome. Steve said at the table, "We would bring up this child and give him the life that he deserves. I do believe that he is our blessing from God, and we're gonna make sure that his blessing to us is taken good care of. I'll make some arrangements next week. Let's just let this little fella relax and play."

Steve had so many high-powered friends and some were pediatricians, one of which he called to come and check the baby out. Others included big-named judges and other lawmakers he would have to count on because now they have a new son in the Bennett home, and he was going to need adoption papers drawn up. Steve knew that he could manipulate the offices that handled that sort of thing due to his high political position.

While sitting at the table, Jean was tending to the little guy as Hazel brought some tea to Steve and Jean. Hazel says to the couple, "What is his name?"

Jean looked over to Steve and said to him, "Let's name him Elliot Thomas Bennett."

Steve said, "Sure," and Hazel looked on and agreed. Elliot Thomas just happened to be the name that they had picked if they were to have a son of their own. That was the name of Jean's grandfather who was killed in war. So then little Mitchell became Elliot Thomas.

Four days had passed, and Bruce received a call at home. The boss allowed him to take some time off after the tragic accident. The person on the phone was the funeral home in Valdosta. They told him that the body of his wife had arrived and he could come down and make funeral and burial arrangements. Bruce agreed, and he told them that he would be there within the hour.

UNINTENTIONALLY CONNECTED

Bruce called his aunt because she still had little Misty, and he just wanted to check on her as well. Bruce really felt numb and weak still. He basically was still in shock from that horrible accident.

As Bruce was getting ready to go to the funeral home, the phone rang. It was one of the investigators covering the accident. He told Bruce that he hated to inform him, but they found a blue baby blanket that was located on the side of the creek, forty yards from where the bus landed. He told Bruce that the blanket was covered in blood and that they were continuing their investigation of the scene but discontinuing a search party for the infant. Bruce then just collapsed on the floor, crying and screaming, "Why, Lord? Why?"

After about two hours later, he then went to make the arrangements for the funeral.

Ten days had passed since the accident. It's the day of Leatha's funeral. Bruce, still numbed, had to borrow so much money to have her put away nicely. The black car pulled up to pick up Bruce, Misty, and some of the family members that had gathered at the house. They arrived at the church, and the choir was singing a song that Bruce wrote. He broke down so bad that another family member had to hold Misty. Even though Misty didn't understand what was going on, she started to cry as well because of all the noise and as she saw her daddy was agitated.

Bruce had to arrange a closed casket funeral because of Leatha's badly burned and charred body. So they set up pictures by the casket, and he also set up pictures of little Mitchell next to Leatha's.

The funeral was very sad. People were breaking down and screaming because the music was so touching. The pastor gave an excellent eulogy for both Leatha and Mitchell. When they arrived at the cemetery, they placed the casket into the ground, and Bruce stayed and watched. He looked like a ghost. He had also arranged the tombstone to include both Leatha and Mitchell's names: LEATHA MARIE WILSON 08/22/1959 to 11/10/1982. Loving wife and mother. MITCHELL DAVID WILSON 09/23/1982 to 11/10/1982.

Everyone saw the tombstone on the grave and just walked quietly back to their cars and left. It was truly the saddest moment in Bruce's life. Everyone went back to the church where the sisters had prepared a very nice meal for everyone. Bruce mingled with everyone, and then he and Misty left the church building and headed to the truck. He looked at Misty while strapping her in the car seat and said, "Baby girl, it's just me and you now, and I'm going to try my best to be everything you need. And whatever you want or wherever you want to go in life, I'll be there to support you. Daddy loves you so much." Tears rolled down his face. He got in the truck on the other side, and they pulled off into the sunset as they headed home.

Seven years had passed since that horrible accident, and Bruce was up, cooking Sunday morning breakfast. Bruce often thought of his morning and evening walks with Roscoe because Roscoe died from old age a few years ago. Little Misty was walking into the kitchen, and she's singing along with the radio that Bruce had playing. He had the gospel station playing, and Misty knew one of the songs. She was a very good singer for a little girl. She loved to sing with her dad in the choir. She was really good in school as well. She was on the honor roll, into sports, and the glee club. She often asked about her mother and brother. Bruce would always tell her that "Mommy and Mitch are in heaven, and they are looking down on you with God." It comforted her when she would become very sad from missing them. She was so little when the accident happened that she couldn't remember any of it. Bruce would take Misty out to the cemetery ever so often to visit where, he told her, Mommy and Mitch lie.

It was time to eat breakfast, and before they eat, they always said their prayers and thanked God for their blessings.

Bruce had learned to do his little daughter's hair and dress her. He was playing both roles now of mother and father. He didn't allow anyone to come into their relationship because he was out to protect his daughter. He did end up dating again, but nothing too serious. His main focus was raising his daughter. She was daddy's little girl.

In church, it was time for the choir to sing, and little Misty was doing her first solo that morning. Bruce was on the organ, and Misty started to sing her little heart out. She was a really gifted singer. She must have gotten it from her daddy. At least that's what Bruce would tell everyone. After service, Misty and Bruce picked up some chicken and were on the way home to eat. They had a wonderful time at church. The church gave Misty a standing ovation for her song, and she just enjoyed it. They walk into the house, and Bruce helped his little girl get her little dress off so she can put on her play clothes. As she lifted her dress up a little, Bruce noticed her foot-shaped birthmark. This automatically reminded him of Mitch. The twins shared the exact same foot-shaped birthmark. It was the same area on the back. That's the only thing they shared that was identical as they were fraternal twins. He gets her play clothes on, and they headed to the kitchen for a big Sunday dinner.

After dinner, Misty asked Bruce if she could go outside to play with her friends. Bruce told her to go on outside but to stay in front of the house. As she went out of the door, her little friends were on the porch, waiting for her. They all had dolls and little girl toys. Bruce thought to himself that it was so cute.

While she was outside, Bruce went into Misty's bedroom. He just stared at the side of the room where Mitchell slept. He saw the crib in his mind as if was still there. Once again, the tears started to roll down his face. He then walked out and entered the den to watch the Braves game on the television set.

Bruce and Misty were doing pretty well. The life insurance policy that Leatha had really helped in buying the house. Bruce also has another car. He had since caught up on all of his bills. Although he was still putting in the hours at work, he had good babysitters for Misty, and he still was able to spend good quality time with his daughter. Bruce, kicked up his legs and relaxed while watching the television and listening to the girls on the porch.

Two months later, Bruce was getting Misty ready to go over to the church for rehearsal. Misty had a recital coming up in a few weeks, and she had to practice, and plus, Bruce had to introduce a new song to the choir.

At the Bennett household, everything was going just perfectly. Jean was finally a true mom to a sweet little boy. Elliot, now seven years old, was upstairs, playing with his trucks as he ran downstairs to see if he can have some cookies. Elliot also picked up a new nickname. E.T. was what the family started calling him. Jean told him that he could have some cookies, so E.T. grabbed his cookies and ran back upstairs to finish playing. Jean also noticed that as he played with his toys, he was singing some song he heard either on the radio or the television. Jean realized that her son had a nice little voice on him. She also noticed how he was really getting to be a solid little fella. He was always eating snacks, and he would always finish his food at every sitting.

Jean has mentally let go of all the negative feelings that she had about how they acquired little E.T. from that horrible accident. She and Steve knew that it was very wrong, how they acquired the funny and cute little boy. Steve had to forge tons of paperwork and lie to so many people to make it happen. They felt that to make a wrong a right so that they would give him the best life possible and make sure that he can get the best education and best medical care. E.T. had asthma. Jean and Steve actually believed that his parents died in the accident and that he probably would be put into the system or given to a family member who may not give him what he needs.

Steve pulled up to the house and little E.T. ran downstairs to see his dad. He loved when daddy would come home because he always brought candy or a toy for him to play with. He ran to the door, saying, "Hi, Daddy! Hi, Daddy! Hi, Daddy!"

Steve brought home a football. E.T. jumped into his arms, and they went outside to throw the football. Little E.T. could barely hold it, but he tried his best to toss it to his dad. Hazel was standing in the door, yelling, "Throw it, E.T.! Throw it as hard as you can!" E.T. looked at Hazel and waved.

E.T. and Hazel also had a wonderful relationship. She often bathed and fed little E.T., and they would play together. Hazel and Jean would read to little E.T. every night until he went to sleep.

Steve told Jean, Hazel, and little E.T. to get ready because he was taking them to a very nice dinner and then to a movie. The family often did that every other weekend. Family time was very important in the Bennett household. E.T. wanted to bring his football, so Steve said fine.

The twins entered into their junior year of high school. Misty attended Valdosta High School. She excelled academically. She was a member of the glee club and stage band, and due to how pretty and petite she was, the cheer team coach insisted that she become a cheerleader. Misty was also very popular around the school and the city. She's known for her singing, piano skills, looks, and personality.

It's the start of the new school year, and Misty has to go down to the school and pick up her uniform for cheerleading. She arrived at the gym, and she saw the team out in the parking lot getting ready to board the bus to football camp. She's had her eye on one of the players for a little while now. He happened to play linebacker for Valdosta and was also a junior that year. She got into the gym, and she saw all the other cheerleaders and also the girls who were trying out. She also saw some of the band members getting sized up for their uniforms as well. They also had a band camp to go to, so there were several busses out in the parking lot. Her coach gave her, her uniform and asked her if she could stay and help out with choosing the new cheerleaders and help them get situated. Misty replied, "Sure, I will."

While watching the new girls did their cheers and flips, Misty was excited because these new girls could really go. There were only two seniors on the squad that year, and they were really close to Misty. Usually, seniors had a stuck-up attitude but those girls were cool with her because they were aware of her popularity and social status. The cheer coach asked Misty to go to the athletic department office to gather a yellow folder with the medical releases in it and bring it to her. Misty went into the office, and she found the folder, but as she was leaving the office, she saw the new football schedule on the wall. She saw a team from Macon, which usually wasn't on their schedule. It was Macon Southwest High School. It was to be Valdosta's second game. She knew the rest of the teams because they were teams that they played every year. She went to the cheer coach and asked her,

"Why are we playing that school from Macon?" The cheer coach explained to her that the team from Macon was really good last year. She explained that Valdosta had the best high school football program in the country so they sometimes have to play the best in the area. She told her that that team had a player who was in the media every week last year as a sophomore and that it was unheard of.

So Misty thought nothing of it, and she went on watching the new cheerleaders. They were really excited about this year's squad.

Misty got home from school as her dad was pulling up as well. Bruce has since moved out to a new home not far from the Five Point Center in Valdosta. He has moved up in his job. He's now a supervisor, and he has a company truck. He bought Misty a little used compact car, so she can get around town and back and forth to school. She was very responsible.

Bruce walked into the house, and Misty was right behind him. He was really tired, so he told Misty that he would cook dinner in a few hours, but he was going to lie down because of the headache he had. She said, "Okay, Dad." She told him that she was going to a friend's house. She asked him if he wanted anything, and he told her no. He lay down across the bed, and Misty left. She's worried about her dad. He had been complaining about headaches a lot more often these days.

It was noon, on Wednesday, a few days before the first day of school. The Valdosta High School football team was hungry for that season. The coaches called for a mandatory meeting of all football team members, cheering squad, and all the band members. The head football coach wanted to encourage all teams and the coaching staff to have a great season. He explained that that year's schedule was going to be a tough one, but of course, Valdosta would prevail. His only concern was Lowndes County because they had an amazing defense that year, and he mentioned Macon Southwest High School because of their offense led by the amazing running back. Those were the coaches' only worries.

UNINTENTIONALLY CONNECTED

So after the speech by the coach, the whole gym that was filled with all teams started chanting, "Wildcats number one," over and over again. Everyone was excited.

It was a very hot day at the Southwest High School football field. The coaches were really pushing the team and running them to death. The offense was running some of their plays, and the coach looked at number 5 and told him to come out for a minute. Number 5 just happened to be E.T. He had grown into a very nice-looking young man. He was very physically fit. He hadn't had an asthma attack in years. He was the star running back that everyone at Valdosta was talking about.

E.T. was just a junior, but he had offers already to go to several colleges to play football. He was very smart. He was also an excellent singer. He played in the concert band when football season was over. He also had all the high school girls wanting to be his girlfriend. E.T. was really soft spoken but a monster on the football field. He was really eager to play Valdosta that year because it was the best team in the land, and he wanted to just destroy their defense and destroy Valdosta's record. That's all he dreamed and thought about. He said to himself, There's just something about this place, but I can't explain it."

The time for practice ended, and E.T. got in his car to go to a friend's house. Before he could pull off, one of the cheerleaders ran to the window an invited him to her house because her parents were not going to be home. E.T. just said that he was sort of busy and that he would call her. She said, "Fine, but call me. I want to see you." He chuckled and pulled off. He reached his friend's house, and they head off to the arcade.

The following Friday, school had been going for a week. It's Southwest High football team's first home game. Steve, Jean, and Hazel were all in the audience. E.T. was running that football like a maniac. He had 325 yards rushing and caught two touchdown passes. He even threw a touchdown pass. They beat a team from Atlanta 56–17. Once again, E.T. was in all the papers in the state of Georgia. After the game, E.T. showered and dressed. The family was waiting in the parking lot. Steve would always take his family to dinner after the Friday home games.

This performance got back to the coaches at Valdosta the next day. They knew that the Southwest team was for real and that it was going to be Valdosta's next game. Valdosta had also won their opener 21–20. Close game but they prevailed.

While at dinner, E.T. told Steve that he had a weird feeling about playing Valdosta. He said, "Dad, there is something about Valdosta. I can feel it, but I just can't pinpoint it."

Steve told him, "Son, don't worry about that feeling. You just go in there, and you run them over." As Steve told him this, Jean and Hazel looked at each other in shock. At that moment, they realized how they took E.T. from that accident that was very close to Valdosta. E.T. told his family that he would do his best.

On Friday morning, school was about to start at Southwest. E.T. was in class and some of the other football team was in there as well. The teacher gave out a pop quiz, but E.T. couldn't really concentrate because his mind was wondering about the game at Valdosta later that evening. The teacher knew something was troubling E.T., so the teacher asked E.T. to come out of the class to talk to him. E.T. went into the hall, and he told the teacher that he was kind of worried about the game that night. He explained to the teacher he had this weird feeling about playing Valdosta. The teacher told him to just do his best and to remember that it would be the night to shine. "So many college recruiters would be there at this game to see how you perform against a number one defense." E.T. thought about it and thanked the teacher. He went back in an aced his quiz.

Then it was time for the teams to board the busses and head for Valdosta. The band had a bus, the pep squad had a bus, and the cheer team rode in one of the two busses for the football team. The team was all chanting, "Beat Valdosta, beat Valdosta." E.T. wasn't saying anything. He just can't get that feeling out of his mind about playing there. It almost felt like he had been there before, but couldn't picture it.

UNINTENTIONALLY CONNECTED

Meanwhile, the Valdosta team was preparing for the game as well. The coaches had all said to the team time and time again, "Stop number 5. Don't let E. Bennett get a single yard."

Valdosta's stadium was packed. It's really loud too. This city had been waiting on this phenomenal team from Macon to show up and get a beating form the Wildcats.

The cheer team was at the entrance where the host team was to enter. Steve, Jean, and Hazel were all sitting over in the visitor's stands along with the majority of the Southwest High School body. On the home side sat Bruce and other family members to watch Misty cheer and for Valdosta destroy this team.

Then came the Southwest team. They got off the bus and headed to the field. They were already dressed, and they were walking right pass the Valdosta cheer team. E.T. passed by Misty and made eye contact. They sort of stared at each other for what seemed like an hour when it was only a shorten ten seconds. E.T. then took to the field while some of the Valdosta cheerleaders were telling Misty, "Girl, he is fine as hell, and he was checking you out. You better get with that."

She started laughing and told them jokingly, "He can't hang with this."

It was game time, and Southwest got the ball first. Valdosta kicked to one of the receivers and the receiver took off. He didn't get but a few yards because of the very hyped defense of Valdosta. Then came the offense and number 5. The whole stadium was going crazy. They wanted to see what this E. Bennett guy was all about. The first play was a hand off to E.T. He cut through the inside, and he broke free. He ran fifty yards before getting tripped up at Valdosta's twenty yard line. The stadium was absolutely stunned. The visitor's side was cheering their hearts out. On the next play's handoff to E.T., he went for the touchdown. Southwest led 7–0 after the field goal.

Bruce leaned over to a buddy of his and said, "That looked like me back in the day." Even Misty was stunned but became more curious of who the guy was.

The game continued, and E.T. just destroyed Valdosta's defense. He ended up with over 250 yards rushing and two touchdowns although Valdosta won the game 21–28 because of their offense. They just couldn't stop E.T. As the game ended, the players were all in the line to shake hands, including the cheerleaders. And when E.T. shook Misty's hand, he held it for a few more seconds than normal. They didn't realize that they were actually fraternal twins who had been separated. Instead, they had more of an erotic stare at each other. E.T. simply said hi, and Misty giggled.

The Southwest High School football team boarded the busses to go back to Macon. On the bus, E.T. couldn't get this girl out of his mind. He was normally talkative and playful on the busses on the way home from a game even after a loss, but this time, he couldn't get that girl out of his mind. He didn't get her name, number, or nothing.

Misty was on her way to meet her dad and her family in the parking lot. She just couldn't get that touch out of her mind. All she thought about was that firm grip and soft voice. Bruce and the rest of her family congratulated her on an excellent performance and good game. They all were headed to get some ice cream. It was a tradition for the Wilsons to go get ice cream after a winning home game.

Throughout the school year the twins would think about that meeting that they had at that high school football game. Both of them would stay up at night, wondering, Who was that?

Soon it was time for graduation. A whole year and a half had passed since the first interaction between the twins. They both have lived life like any normal teenager, and they have gone through the ups and downs and had heartbreaks and falling in puppy love. Now they're off to enter the world of adulthood. They both have made decisions of what to do after high school graduation.

At the Wilson's household, Misty was getting ready for graduation. She's in her room, putting on her makeup. As she was applying her lipstick, Bruce walked in, and he sat on the bed next to her, and he told her how he was so proud of her. There was only one thing that he didn't agree with and that was the fact the Misty had entered into the United States Navy for four years. She knew that Bruce couldn't afford for her to go to college, and she really wanted to make it on her own. She was due to leave in just one week after graduation. Although Bruce didn't agree with that decision, he had to support her because she was making a decision about her life that she was responsible for.

Bruce walked over to her, and he told her that he loved her so much, and he wished that her mom was there to celebrate and he also wished that her twin brother was graduating as well. He told her that God had a better plan for them. Bruce was crying as he told her this. Misty started crying as well. She didn't know her mom or brother, but she often told Bruce that she felt their presence with her a lot. She also told Bruce that she felt that her brother was right next to her at times.

Misty was now getting ready to go across the stage and receive her diploma, and she started to walk when she felt a breeze brush across her face, and she says under her breath, "Thank you, Mama. Thank you, Mitchell." She grabbed her diploma, and she was on her way.

Elliot was getting ready for his graduation. His graduation just happened to be a few days after Misty's. Steve, Jean, and Hazel were all in the car, headed to the auditorium. While Steve was parked the car, they all got out. Steve pulled Elliot to the side, and he said, "Son, I am so proud of you, and me and your mom really love you. You have been a blessing to everyone you've come into contact with."

Elliot had accepted a football scholarship to the US Naval Academy. He was to play for four years and would become a naval officer after four years. And then after his contract, he had the option to go pro if he chose to.

They called Elliot's name to receive his diploma, and he walked across the floor. The entire auditorium was up, cheering. Elliot was extremely popular because he was the best football player in the state. He was also a scholar, and he had a wonderful personality to go along with all of his accolades.

Misty just graduated from naval recruit training in Illinois and successfully completed the dental tech school. She was now to report to the naval hospital in Bethesda for her first two years. Misty was very excited, and she really looked forward to this transition. She also knew that they only sent the best sailors to Bethesda and that this is where the president receives his treatment as well as other high-powered dignitaries.

While in Bethesda, Misty settled in, and she purchased a small apartment not far from the base. She was starting to meet friends and now starting to hang out in Washington's nightlife. She would often call her dad to check on him. She knew her dad wasn't in the best of health. He was really coughing a lot when she talked with him last. She often sent him cards by mail when she can. She did on occasion and even many of the officers would try and hit on her. In the military, that's grounds for court martial. Fraternizing was frowned upon in the military. She was so pretty that the officers didn't care.

It was September, and she had a patient in the chair that was waiting on a cleaning. In some of the rooms of that naval dental clinic, there were televisions suspended from the ceiling. As she's working on a patient, the patient wanted to watch the football game. So Misty turned on the television, and she started back her cleaning on this patient's mouth. She noticed that he had a cavity that needed to be filled. So Misty grabbed the dentist. He was a commander in the navy. He enjoyed watching football as well. It just so happened that the Naval Academy was playing Georgia Tech that day. Not paying attention to the television, the commander and Misty started to work on the patient. The announcer yelled excitedly, "Its Elliot Bennett for the touchdown. What an exceptional run by the freshman running back." She immediately took her attention off the patient and stared at the television. She had heard that name before. It took a minute, but she remembered exactly where she heard it. It was from her junior year in high school at the football game. It was the guy who touched her, and whom she had dreamed about for months.

The commander was telling her to grab one of the dental instruments, and she was in a daze and didn't pay him any attention, so he said it again loudly, and she said, "Oh! Oh, okay, sir. I'm sorry." He said that's fine, but he explained to her to be more focused on her job.

Later that evening, Misty got off her job, and she went back to her apartment. Some of her girlfriends were coming by to go out that night. They loved the weekends in DC because there was so much going on. It was much livelier than living in Valdosta. So her girlfriend's came by, and they went out to a club to hang for the night. All while they were out, she couldn't get Elliot out of her mind. She still remembered that touch at the game two years ago.

Elliot was once again the star of the football squad at the academy. He was breaking all the freshman records there. He was really focused on the NFL. He had calls from some of the coaches, which were illegal according to NCAA rules. They called him anyway. He was just that good. His dad, Steve, would sometimes fly up to some of his games. Elliot was at the mall, buying some clothes. He was looking at just buying a pair of jeans as he took the jeans to the dressing room to try them on when a girl snuck in the back with him. She managed to get through the door before he could close it. She told him that she thought that he was the finest thing she had ever seen and that she wanted him. She started to take her top off and caressed him. Elliot stopped her and said that he was very dedicated to his girlfriend and that he couldn't do that. So he politely pushed her out of the door. She yelled some obscenities and made obscene gestures at him. He just continued to try on his new jeans. E.T. did have a girlfriend back in Macon, but it was nothing too serious. He was very respectful to himself and to others. That was the teaching that Steve and Jean taught him. He bought his blue jeans and started walking back in the mall. He glanced over at a display in a woman's store. He actually looked through the glass into the store, and there was a girl that looked exactly like that girl he remembered at that high school football game. So he turned to walk into the store to see if it could be her, but of course it wasn't. This girl looked somewhat like her but she had two kids with her, and she was cussing and acting like a fool. She was really ghetto. So he continued on his way. He realized that this girl, whoever she was, was still on his mind. He couldn't figure out why.

It was time for Misty to decide where she wanted to pick her next duty station. A couple of things have come to her mind. She really didn't want to go on a ship, but she didn't have to worry about that due to women, at that time, were only on hospital ships. So she put in that she wanted to go to Mayport to work in the dental clinic. There she will be close to Valdosta, and she could check on her dad, who still wasn't doing too well. She put in her request, and she had to wait a few days before she heard anything.

A few days went by, and she finally got the news back that she wanted. She was to report to Mayport in thirty days. She was so excited. She had been in the navy for two years, and she had just been having the time of her life. Soon she could be near her dad, and she can check on him more often.

She arrived at Mayport, and she was amazed at the large ships that were in port at that time. She was really excited. She checked in at the gate, and they gave her instructions as to where to go. She said to herself, "This is home for a while."

She just happened to be staying in the barracks on the base, so she won't be able to get an apartment for a while. She met another female sailor, Sara, who just happened to be a hospital corpsman. They sort of work side by side, and she told Misty that she would show her the ropes. After a day of going over the base and showing the ins and outs of the clinic, they went to the barracks and changed and went out in Jacksonville. Jacksonville was a beautiful city. They loved the Jacksonville Landing. It's a riverfront spot with shops, restaurants, and clubs. Misty was finally settled in, and she loved the place.

It had been two years, and Misty was up for reenlistment. She would choose to do so if she could stay in Mayport. The captain pulled some strings for her because she was an excellent dental tech and person. She already reached E4, and she was on her way to becoming a chief petty officer if she chose to. She just had to continue doing a good job for another four years.

Meanwhile back at the academy, Elliot continued to be a true star. He would break records and help take his team to a bowl game every year. He graduated from the academy, and he received his first set of orders. By coincidence, his orders led him to Mayport. He was to report to a ship there where he will be a lieutenant. His degree was in accounting. He will be working in the administrative department of the ship.

Elliot was happy about this cause he wasn't far from home, and he could get back and check on his parents. Although he wanted to go pro, but due to his commitment, he had to serve out his military contract. All the NFL teams were looking at him, but he had to fulfill his obligation. The Chicago Bears were really trying to acquire him. Elliot sustained a minor knee injury in his last year that sidelined him for several games. That sort of put a dark cloud over his future draft potential.

Right after graduation, Elliot had thirty days before reporting to Mayport. He relaxed at home with his family and just did odd jobs around the big house for his parents. He and Hazel would often play chess, and she would beat him all the time. One day at the dinner table, Elliot broke down and humbly told his parents and Hazel how much he was so thankful at how they have raised him and given him everything a kid could ever ask for. Elliot knew he was adopted, but he never mentioned or asked, out of curiosity, what happened to his parents and/or blood relatives. He had a wonderful upbringing, and he really expressed that to his parents.

Steve brought up an idea, he told the family, "For old time's sake, let's eat dinner and let's all go to the movies." So they did as a family.

On the way to the movies, Steve explained to Elliot that he would be retiring soon, and he was excited about that. He told Eliot that he was thinking of running for office, but it was sort of too late for him to do so. They saw a great movie and returned home to dessert made by Hazel, hot fudge sundaes, and they all just chowed it down.

That Saturday, Elliot packed his things in his car and got ready to hit the road for Mayport. He was to report on Monday, but he was going to spend a day in Jacksonville and check out the town. He kissed his mom, Hazel, and then his dad good. He told all three that he loved them and he drives off in his own BMW that Steve bought him as a graduation present.

Driving south on I-75, Elliot is listening to soft music and he's singing. He saw the sign Valdosta 20 miles. Immediately, he started thinking about that girl at the game. He often wondered who she was and where could she be. None of the other girls he'd dated has had that weird impact on him like that.

After a few hours, he finally reached Jacksonville, and he was amazed at all the bridges there. The city was beautiful. He was going to be staying downtown at a very nice hotel that his dad had arranged for him to stay. Steve didn't want his boy staying at any dump, so he made arrangements for him to stay at an exclusive hotel.

Elliot pulled up to the hotel, and the attendant took his bags to the counter. The parking attendant took his keys and parked his car for him. He's being treated like he was a movie star or a big-named athlete.

Elliot checked in to his hotel, and he went into his room and lay down to take a nap. After a few hours of sleep, he woke up, and he's ready to go out into the streets. He just didn't know where to go. After he showered and puts on his fresh clothes he headed downstairs.

He went to the service desk and asked the attendant on duty, "What're the happening spots out here in J town?"

The attendant asked him what he liked to do, and Eliot replied that he was open to whatever. He just wanted to get out into the Jacksonville nightlife. So the attendant said that there is the new thing going on, and it's called karaoke. Eliot didn't know what that was so he asked him, "What's that?" The attendant explained to him that it was a club setting where people can get up to sing to a song with the words on a screen and have their five minutes of fame. "You get up there, whether you can sing or not, and do whatever song you desire."

Elliot thought about that. It was weird to him, but it caught his interest because he could really sing. He asked the attendant for directions, and Elliot was on his way.

He pulled up, and there was a small crowd gathered at the door to get in. He parked his new BMW that is now starting to cause attention among the ladies. He went in, and amazingly, it was free to get in. He went up to the bar, and he was amazed at all the people that were in there, watching each other got up to a mike and sing. He ordered a drink, and the barmaid offered him a song book to look at. It was filled with songs from all types of styles and time periods. He couldn't figure out how they played the song, but there wasn't anyone singing behind it, only the person up at the mike. Well, he knew that he could sing, so he looked through this book for some songs, and he found something that he knew that he could sing really well. It was a Boyz II Men song, "End of the Road." He walked up and gave the slip to the karaoke host and went back to the bar and waited his turn. He was amazed at all the different singers in there. Some were really good singers, but the majority of the singers were horrible, but it didn't matter because they were out to have fun.

Little did Elliot realize but Misty and her girlfriends pulled up outside, and they parked and got in. Misty and her friends had been singing here for some time. Misty was an excellent singer. She always roused the crowd, and she was often there every weekend unless she had to serve watch duty at the base.

Misty and her four girlfriends sat at a table closer to the front of the club. They were all having a good time. The waiter brought their drinks, and Misty and another friend of hers put their names in to sing. Elliot was at the bar making small talk with some of the people that were sitting at there. He saw Misty walk by with her friends. He couldn't recognize her because it was dark in the club and also as it had been some years since he had seen her last. She made eye contact with him as well, but she immediately looked away. When she last saw Elliot, he had his football helmet on, so she wouldn't have recognized him anyway.

The host called E.T. to the stage. Eliot wrote E.T. on his slip because that was his nickname while growing up in Macon. It was short for Elliot Thomas.

Everyone was clapping as he started singing, then everyone got really quiet as they all listened to that wonderful voice that he had. Elliot tore that song apart. He was really making it his own. He also was making quite a few fans in the meantime.

Misty and her girlfriends were really amazed. As Misty watched him perform on that stage, she never would have thought that that guy was her twin brother. What were the chances? She was telling her girlfriends of how sexy he was, and her girlfriend Sara said that she wanted to take him home.

As Elliot got off the stage, everyone in the club were clapping and cheering really hard. The bartender had a policy that if you get a big cheer like that, he would send a free drink to you. Well, Elliot got his free drink as well as a lot of compliments. He still remained at the bar alone.

Now, Sara's name was called, and she got up to do an old song from Fleetwood Mac called "Dreams." She did okay, but the crowd wasn't into her singing. She was not a stand out like Elliot. Elliot was there at the bar, watching on and having a blast. Next up was Misty. Immediately, she got the attention of everyone in the club. She chose a song by Mariah Carey, and Misty started singing, and the whole place went nuts. She had a voice that was out of this world. Elliot was amazed at her talent. When she got off the stage, the crowd was going wild. Even Elliot had to get off of his barstool and clap for that amazing voice and the beautiful young lady that voice came from. So time went on, and it was getting late. Elliot got up from the bar as he paid his tab. As he walked toward the door Sarah, came from behind him and introduced herself, and she asked if he would come to the table with her before he leaves. Elliot didn't mind, so he said okay.

He got over to the table with the girls, and they all said hello and what an amazing job he did, singing. Misty was asking him if he had any training in singing. He said no. He introduced himself as E.T. They didn't think anything of it because all of the girls were a little tipsy anyway. He sat down for another drink even though he had just paid his tab. The girls started talking military stories, and they informed Elliot that they were in the navy, and they were stationed over at the Mayport naval base. Elliot told them that he was reporting to duty on Monday morning. Misty got really excited. The other girls were checking out Elliot's physic more than anything. Misty told Elliot that he would really love this base. Elliot offered to buy the girls a round of drinks before he left. He never was a real big partier, so he never really stayed out late.

Another half an hour went pass, and the girls and Elliot continued to laugh at the other singers and have a good time. Misty asked Elliot what E.T. stood for, and he told her that was his nickname growing up and that he really didn't want to give out his name in public to people he didn't know. She looked at him like. "Oh! Big time, huh?" He said no, but he didn't know any of those people. Once again as he talked, Misty just continued to stare at him.

The barmaid brought the check to the table, and Elliot grabbed it and said, "I got it." The girls were so thankful. He pulled out his credit card, and the barmaid took it up to the cashier. She came back and gave him the slip. Eliot signed it and tipped her. The barmaid read the tip and said, "Thank you, Elliot."

Misty glanced at the slip, and she finally saw his name. In her mind she was saying, It's him. It's him. OMG. She almost fell from the chair. She immediately asked, "Did you live in Macon, Georgia?" He said yes. Then she asked, "Are you that football player that wore number 5 who came to Valdosta and ran all over us?" He said yes. While she's telling him that, he started getting excited because now he knew it was that girl who he held hands with at the high school game, and the girl he had longed to find where her whereabouts was.

Both of them jumped up and hugged each other very tightly. As they sat back down, they remained holding hands.

They started asking each other question after question about what they have been doing since that meeting between them. Elliot cracked a joke, saying that she was the reason that he didn't do better in that game because he had his eye on her. Misty laughed. Misty asked if he played at the academy as well, and he said yes.

The more he talked, the more Misty was getting excited and wanted to be with him. Again, she would have never known that that nice-looking guy was actually her fraternal twin brother.

The club was about to close, and it was really late. Misty and Elliot were still continuing their talk. The girls were on their way back to the car, so Misty asked when she could see him again. Elliot told her that he didn't have a phone number yet because he was just reporting to the base on Monday. So Misty gave him the number to the barracks where she was staying and also her cell. She knew that he was an officer because he graduated from the academy. She knew the harsh trouble they both could get in by trying to date him. She threw those thoughts out of her head.

Misty told Elliot to call her the next day, so they could talk and possibly meet up for brunch or something. Elliot said that he would.

It was Sunday morning, and it's around six thirty in the morning. Elliot went down to the hotel's gym to get a good workout in. He worked out about an hour. He then went back to his room and showered then got dressed and went to breakfast. He didn't want to call Misty so early. He figured that she was still sleeping or something because they had a really long night.

He had a good, filling breakfast then he headed back to his room to call Misty. He didn't want to call her cell because if she was working, she could get in trouble for having a cell phone in her work area. He dialed the number and it rang five times before someone picked up. He asked if he could he speak to Misty. The girl that answered the phone gave the phone to Misty, and she just smiled and they talk for the next two hours. While on the phone Misty, told Elliot that she was very hungry, so Elliot offered to take her to a late lunch, but he told her that he didn't know his way around Jacksonville. She offered to pick him up from his hotel. He agreed. He gave her the name of the hotel, and she was on her way.

She arrived at the hotel, and Elliot just happened to be down in the lobby. So he got in the car, and they drove off. The first stop was to get a burger because Misty said she was so hungry. They decided to go to Sonics. They could drive up and eat right there in the car.

After they ordered and had eaten their food, Misty asked him if he was excited about his first day the next day. He told her that he was. She also explained that she was enlisted and that he was an officer. Elliot knew the consequences of that, but he told her that they were just friends anyway, so what were they going to say?

They got tired of sitting at Sonics, so Misty then drove to the beach area where she showed him how beautiful Jacksonville was. She parked in a parking lot near the beach, and off they went walking, arriving at the beach holding hands.

Misty started telling her life story about how she had a brother and a mother who died in an awful bus accident when she was just an infant. She told of how her father raised her. She explained of how she wished that her mom and brother could be in her life at that point. She really poured her heart out to Elliot.

He also told of his background. How he was adopted and that he never knew his natural parents and that he didn't want to anyway because of how good his adoptive parents were to him. He told her that he was an only child and how lonely it got sometimes not having anyone to play with.

They shared stories for three hours, just walking up and down the beach. It was late and Elliot said that he had a big day ahead of him the next day, so he'd better get back to the room to get his rest. Misty explained that they had 6:00 a.m. muster as well.

On the way back to Elliot's hotel, they decided to get another bite to eat, and so that time, they went inside and ate. It was a smorgasbord-type dinner, which they both enjoyed. They left, and it was off to the hotel. Elliot said that it felt weird having a woman dropped him off at a hotel instead of it being the other way around. As Misty pulled up to the front, Elliott reached over and kissed her on the cheek. Misty said, "Wait a minute." She put the car in the park, and she gave him the deepest, most passionate kiss ever. It was very intense. They stopped and stared at each other for a moment then Elliot said that he had to go and that he would call her once he checked in at the base. She said, "Fine." He got out and she drove off.

On the way, she couldn't stop thinking about how they found each other. It was almost as though fate had planned this union. They still had no idea that they were actually fraternal twins. It was really weird that neither twin was romantically involved with any other person at that point.

On Monday morning, Elliott was looking sharp in his khaki officer uniform. As he arrived at the base and then on to the aircraft carrier, all of the sailors saluted him. He enjoyed that. While getting checked in and settled on his ship, Elliott cannot stop thinking about the time that he spent with Misty. He would sometimes go into a stupor, reminiscing about how she touched him, how passionately she kissed him as well as about more of deeper erotic acts.

The captain showed Elliot around the ship, his sleeping quarters, where the officer's mess hall was located, and where he would be working. He took him to the flight deck, the hangar deck, and to the medical department. The captain introduced him to several of the senior officers as well as the senior enlisted officers. He then met the crew that he would oversee. Some of them were excited to meet him because they remember him from playing football at the Naval Academy. The captain informed Elliot that the ship was scheduled to go to sea in two weeks for ten days for refresher trials, and he had to make arrangements to store his car in the base.

Elliot was excited about the new journey in his life. He had a lot of responsibility on his shoulders now, and he was also thought about the fact that he just may have a serious relationship in his life now with Misty.

Later in the afternoon, Elliott called Misty's barracks, and Misty's friend answered and told him that Misty had to complete her watch. Elliot left a message with her to give to Misty and it included his new phone number of where he'll be.

It's 6:30 p.m., and Elliott hadn't heard from Misty yet, so he decided to head over to the officer's club for a bite to eat. While walking to get off the ship, so many sailors saluted him because he had his uniform on. Being an officer in uniform meant that the enlisted had to salute him. Elliot didn't unpack because he was so busy; otherwise, he would have removed his uniform and wore shorts or jeans.

The officer's club was a good walking distance from the ship. As Elliot walked, he actually saw Misty and some of her friends walking toward their barracks. They were going to cross his path. Elliot decided to cross the street and walk out of their way to avoid them. He didn't want Misty saluting him because she was in her uniform as well. Misty did see him, and she just stared at him, and she knew what he was doing. They did make eye contact as Elliot got out of their way. He winked at her, and she winked back at him, and they both made their way to their destinations.

Later that evening, they ended up talking on the phone. Elliot asked her if she can handle the fact that she was enlisted and he was an officer. She replied yes. He told her that they would have to be very discreet because they both could get in a lot of trouble. Mayport naval base was so large that it was rare that they would see each other anyway. Plus, by Elliott being on the ship, he would be gone a lot as well.

Elliott did mention to her that the ship was pulling out in two weeks for ten days of REFTRA, which is short for "refresher trials." Sadly, she replied, "Okay." She informed him that she had to make a trip home because her dad was very ill, so Elliot told her that he would go with her to meet her dad.

Two weeks have gone by, and Elliott and Misty had been out a couple of times to eat at restaurants that were very far away due to the fact that they didn't want anyone from the base recognizing them being together. Their relationship was growing, and they were starting to feel very comfortable with each other. To their surprise, they had so much in common. So many of her likes were his likes and vice versa. They enjoyed the same foods, and they even had the same allergies. Again, they just didn't have any idea that they were fraternal twins. They just thought that they both had found someone very special. They actually were falling in love. They really have been having a wonderful time.

It had been three weeks, and Elliott's ship is pulling in. As they docked, all of the electrical lines and phone line to the ship were being hooked up. Elliot immediately called Misty's barracks, but no one answered. He called the dental clinic where she worked, but she wasn't there. Then he had to call her cell phone, and finally, she picked up. She was happy to hear him, but she was crying. She told him that her dad had a stroke, and that she desperately needed to go to Valdosta to see him. It was Friday afternoon. Elliott didn't have any watches that weekend, so he offered to take her. He told her to just give him a few hours to get settled, and he would pick her up at her friend's apartment off base. Still crying, she said okay. They both didn't have to report back till Monday.

Finally, Elliott arrived at the apartment and he jumped out of the car to Misty. She was standing in the front entrance of the apartment building complex. She was crying, and Elliot embraces her and told her let's go. He opened her door, and he put her in the BMW, attached her seatbelt, and he ran to the other side, and they were off to Valdosta.

On the way, Misty told Elliott that her dad was all she had. She lost her mom and brother. She did say that she had a half-brother, but the last she heard of him was that he was in a jail cell somewhere in Ohio. Misty desperately wanted her dad to meet Elliot. She explained how he raised her and taught her so much about life. She also told him of how he really missed his wife and his son.

They arrived in Valdosta, and Misty said, "Let's go directly to the hospital." They pulled into the parking lot and walk to the entrance. Misty explained to Elliott that that was where she and her brother were born. They get the information from the front desk of Bruce's room number, and they proceeded to the elevator. They were the only two on the elevator, and as the doors closed, Misty planted a big kiss on Elliot's lips and told him, "Thank you so much."

Elliot said, "Hon, no problem. This is me. This is what I'm about."

They reached Bruce's room, and other family members were in the room as well. Bruce was hooked to all types of monitors. Misty ran over to her dad in tears. As she did that, Elliot introduced himself to the family members that were there in the room. One of Misty's cousins asked if he was her boyfriend, and without hesitation, Elliot said, "Yes, I am."

Misty heard him while she was hugging her dad, and it soothed her and made her happy even though she couldn't stand seeing her father in that condition. Bruce was able to open his eyes, and he smiled a little. His face drooped, and he appeared to not have any control of movement on his left side. Misty introduced Elliot to him, and Bruce looked toward him and tried to smile. Elliot immediately went to his side and said, "Sir, it is an honor to meet you." Bruce appeared to cry because, out of just one eye, a tear went down his face. He was happy.

They all sat with Bruce in his hospital room for at least three hours, and it was late, so the nurse informed the family that visiting hours were over and that Bruce really needed his rest. The nurse also informed the family that they would be running a series of tests on Bruce within the next couple of days. The family came together and surrounded Bruce's bed, holding hands, and one of Misty's cousins, who was a minister, said a beautiful prayer. Everyone left, and Misty and Elliot headed to the car. Misty had to go by her house, but she didn't want to stay there. She went to grab some items to make sure that everything was intact, and she asked Elliot was it okay if they went and got a hotel room. He said yes.

They ended up getting a hotel there in Valdosta. Bruce paid for it. While walking toward the room, Misty made a joke at Elliot. She told him, "Hey, the last time you were here, you got beat, didn't you?"

Elliot laughed and replied while walking through the door, "Yeah, but this time, I'm going to win," and they both laughed and laughed.

Bruce turned the television on and sat on the bed. Misty immediately jumped on him, kissing him deeply. In the heat of passion, she said she wanted him, and Elliot said that he wanted her. They start to caress each other, and they started kissing. Elliott even suck on her neck and earlobes.

They both come out of their clothes, and they made love passionately over and over. They lay there, holding each other until morning.

They woke up to the morning sunlight shining through the windows. They held each other tightly. Misty kissed Elliot on the forehead and told him that she felt so good being with him. Elliot told her that he has fallen for the Valdosta girl who held his hand. They both showered together and they got dressed. Neither of them ever noticed the birthmark they had in common. They grabbed a quick breakfast and went to see about Bruce.

Bruce had showed no signs of improvement. He couldn't talk or make any other gesture. He could look at you and try and blink, but his stroke was so massive that it paralyzed most of his body. He had tubes in and out of his body and monitors everywhere. As Misty and Elliot arrived, the charge nurse informed Misty that the doctor wanted to talk with the immediate family. Misty said okay. She called her aunt and some of Bruce's cousins and asked them to come to the hospital.

At 3:30 p.m., all the family was gathered together. The doctor came in and told some of the family to meet him in the conference room down the hall. He showed the family the X-ray that was taken of Bruce's brain after the stroke. He said that the percentage of damaged tissue was so severe that he was surprised that Bruce was still alive today. The doctor explained that it was just a matter of time before other mini strokes would start, and then Bruce would fall asleep and never wake up.

Misty took that really hard, and Elliot embraced her very tightly. The rest of the family was very sad. Misty just kept saying, "He's all I got. Daddy can't leave me."

They go back into the room where Bruce was, and he did have his eyes opened a little. He appeared to be happy to see his family because he tried to smile. Bruce appeared to be aware of what was going on around him even though he had had a major stroke. While walking over to Bruce's bedside, Misty dropped an ink pen on the floor. Elliot bent down to pick up the pen, and his backside was facing Bruce. Elliot's shirt was really loose. Bruce glanced over with his eyes barely open and saw Elliot's foot-shaped birthmark on his backside. The family members saw Bruce glance over at Elliot's backside, and they witnessed Bruce getting very agitated. His vital signs were going crazy. Bruce knew that Elliott was his son Mitch. He couldn't communicate to tell anyone. He just kept shaking and trying to point his finger at Elliott. The nurse was called to give him a sedative to calm him down. Misty's cousin made a joke at Elliot and told him that his butt must be ugly because it made Bruce go into convulsions. Everyone laughed a little bit. After the nurse administered the sedative, Bruce fell asleep, and then everyone left.

Misty decided that it would be good to go and visit the gravestone of her mom and brother. She did that quite often. She would go out to the gravesite, sit down by the grave stone and gave a small prayer and have a conversation. She didn't know her mom, but she would talk to the stone as if there were a communication device that led to her mom's ear.

Misty and Elliot headed out toward the cemetery, and on the way, Misty brought up the fact that if her dad passes away, she didn't know what to do with the house and all the other valuables he had. She knew that by her being in the military, she wouldn't be around to take care of all his property. Elliot told her not to worry about it and that everything would be fine. He would make sure of it.

Finally, Elliot pulled up near the gravesite, and they walked over hand in hand. As they got closer, Misty told Elliott that something felt very weird about visiting the grave that day. They reached the headstone, and Elliot read it. He saw her mother's name, and he also noticed that there was another name on the headstone. He asked Misty were both her mom and little twin brother buried together, and she told him no. She said that it was more of a memorial for her brother due to the fact that his body was never found and that her mother was the only occupant of the grave. Elliot asked, "So your brother's name was Mitchell?"

She replied, "Yes."

Elliot said that was a nice name. Elliot had no idea that he was actually visiting a grave that has his original name on it. That grave was actually in memorial of him.

They cleaned the grave off, and Misty, as usual, talked to the headstone as if her mom was actually living. She just asked, "Mom, what do I do about Dad? I don't know what to do." Then she said, "Mitch, I wish you were here to help me make these decisions. I really love you both." She looked at Elliot, and they embraced tightly in front of the gravestone, and then they just quietly walked back to the car hand in hand.

They go back to the hotel room with a pizza that they grabbed on the way to eat, and they took a nap. They were going to go back to the hospital later that evening to spend time with Bruce. They were going to head back to Jacksonville early the next morning. They both didn't have to report back to the naval base until 6:00 a.m. Monday morning the following day.

They have been asleep a couple of hours now. Misty decided that it was about time they headed on over to the hospital to see Bruce. They both got dressed, and they headed over to the hospital.

Elliot decided to stop by a store to pick up some flowers and a get well card and bring them to Bruce. Misty thought that that was the sweetest thing. So they got to the room, and Bruce's eyes were open. Elliot walked in, walked over to the bed, and spoke to Bruce. Elliot touched Bruce's hand and then he put Bruce's flowers and card on the windowsill. Bruce still stared at him, and he tries to say something, but due to the stroke, he can't. Misty went over and kissed him on the forehead. Again Bruce tried to say something to Elliot, and he can't. Bruce even appeared to smile, but he just can't do anything else.

Misty's cousins, Alicia and Erica, arrived at Bruce's hospital room, and they informed Misty not to worry about Bruce's house because they would see about it until they figure out what to do. They were older cousins who grew up with Bruce. They were already taking care of Bruce's property. Misty told them that it was time for them to get back to the room to get some sleep because they were headed back to Jacksonville in the morning.

Misty reached over and kissed Bruce on the forehead, and he smiled. Elliot steps over and rubbed Bruce's hand and told him that he would come and see him whenever he can. They both walked out the door and headed back to the hotel room.

As the night went on, Misty and Bruce lay together, she turned to Bruce and told him, "I wonder why Daddy looked at you so funny when you picked up my pen." She explained to Elliot, "He really got excited when you got that pen for me."

Elliot made a joke, saying, "Maybe he was laughing that my outfit was not matching." They both chuckled, and they went to sleep in each other's arms.

On Sunday morning, Elliot and Misty had been on the road for an hour. Elliot was getting closer to the apartment where Misty's car was parked. Finally, they reached the apartment. Elliot got around and opened Misty's door. Misty got out, carrying her bag. She thanked Elliott for going with her and supporting her during the visit to see her dad. Elliot said that it would never be a problem. He explained that he really liked her family, and he was crazy about her dad. Misty then told him that she really loved making love to him. Elliott said that he enjoyed it as well and that he couldn't wait to see her again. Misty asked Elliot if he was serious when he referred to her as his girlfriend, and Elliott replied, "Yes." He said that he was not playing, and that he was ready for a relationship with her. He told her that she was everything that he was looking for in a mate and that they had so much in common. Misty agreed. They then embraced each other and kissed each other very passionately. Elliot jumped back in the car. He blew kisses at Misty while he pulled off very slowly. He got on the expressway and headed back to the ship.

Elliot arrived at the ship and then called Misty to let her know that he made it safely and that he was headed to his rack to lie down for a while.

After about two hours of napping, Elliot went to the gym to put in a serious workout. He still very much wanted to join the NFL, and after his military obligation, he would be free to sign with any team that wanted him. While working out, he couldn't get his mind off Misty. He really was head over heels about that girl, and he just wanted things to run smoothly. He hadn't told his parents about it yet because his father always instilled in his mind to make sure that his career came first, and when he had settled in his career, then that's the time to think about a relationship. Elliot never really had a lot of girlfriends because he was so busy with sports and his dad was always on his back about not getting a girl pregnant and bringing a disease home. During Elliot's workout, he saw everyone in the gym watching him. Someone put the word out about who he was. That he was that big-time football player who played at the academy, so a lot of the men enlisted and officers were coming over to him for conversation, and some even wanted autographs.

Misty got her car, and she headed back to the base. While driving, she just couldn't stop thinking about Elliot. She really wanted him as a mate. She was thinking to herself how everything was just perfect about him, his conversation, touch, body, his lovemaking skills, and his gentle heart. She reached the base and went to her barracks and lay down for a nap.

At 6:00 a.m. Monday morning, Elliot was doing the uniform inspections of the enlisted personnel in his department. He was now going to be over the administrative division of the ship. Everyone appeared to look decent and in order. The enlisted young men ranged from the ranks of E3 to E6, and they all were a little intimidated by Elliot's physique. Elliot was larger than all of them, more muscular, and he stood about 6 feet 2 inches tall. He was a big-time football player, so he had to be more muscular and built than the average person.

Elliot gave his guys the plan of the day and then he dismissed them. He then went to his desk and sent a text to Misty. The text read, "I can't stop thinking about you, and I cannot wait to see you later. Let's make plans to go to dinner tonight somewhere." She replied after about a fifteen-minute wait, "Yes yes, and I cannot wait to see you, baby."

Later in the day, Elliot received a notice handed to him from the captain himself, and it read that the ship was going to be going out in three weeks for another two weeks, but they would be stopping in St. Thomas, Virgin Island, for a few days of liberty. The ship had to go through more flight ops trials, and then after they had a satisfactory score, they would head back to Mayport. They were preparing for a six-month cruise later in the year, and it was so much preparation to go through first.

Elliot was not excited about the news because he couldn't see leaving Misty right now for that period of time. He knew there was nothing he could do to change that; he just had to deal with it.

Later that evening, Elliot called his parents back in Macon. They were surprised to hear from him. It had been a while, but Elliot explained to them that he had been really busy. His dad told him about this huge case that he just got finished with and how it made the news there in Macon. Hazel even got on the phone and told him that she missed him and missed taking care of him. She told Elliot that she was taking care of Steve and Jean and not to worry about anything. Jean just loved hearing her boy's voice. He then called Misty, and they decided to meet again at Misty's friend's apartment. So Elliot was on his way over there.

He pulls up and Misty just happened to be outside waiting on him, and she has her friend with her. Elliot is kind of nervous getting out of the car because he knows that he and Misty should not be seeing each other due to the fact that he was an officer, and she was enlisted. Misty explained that this was her girl and she was a good friend. She assured him that she wouldn't say anything. Elliot still was feeling scared. He opened Misty's door, and Misty got in. Elliot ran around to his side and jumped in, and he drove off quickly.

Elliott told her again that it was important that they keep their relationship a secret due to the fact that they both could get in serious trouble.

Elliot drove to a drive through restaurant, and they grabbed some burgers. They went to the beach. They ate in the car and talked while the dusk breeze blew through the windows. Elliot explained that he would be going back out to sea in a few weeks and that he didn't want to go. He explained that all he wanted to do was spend time with her.

They finished their burgers and then they went walking on the beach. Again, they were hand in hand, and they often kissed on the path. Then Elliot said, "Let's do something crazy. Let's go to our singing spot over on the north side of Jacksonville." Misty agreed, and even though it was a week night, they still wanted to spend time at the place where they became reacquainted with each other. So they ran side by side back to the car and went to the karaoke spot.

At 10:00 p.m., they arrived at the karaoke club only to find that there were other noticeable navy personnel inside of which a few were in Elliot's department. Misty and Elliot didn't recognize them until they got further inside. So they decided to split up until they could figure something out. Elliot went to the bar, and Misty went to a table. When Misty went to her table, a young navy sailor saw her sat down by herself. Immediately, he told the bartender that he wanted to buy her a drink. So the barmaid went to ask her what she wanted to drink because the young man at the bar wanted to buy her a drink. Misty replied, "Nothing," after she saw who it was. The sailor didn't realize that her man was sitting right next to him at the bar. So Elliot started laughing, and he turned to the bar tender and said "I want to buy that same girl a drink." The barmaid went back out and told Misty that the other gentleman wanted to buy her a drink. The barmaid pointed out Elliot, and she said yes. Misty knew that the sailor was watching them, so she told the barmaid to give him her number. This really made the sailor guy mad, so he got up and went to the other side of the bar. Misty and Elliot looked at each other and laughed.

The singing had started, and there were some horrible singers in the club that night. They were just destroying every song that was chosen.

Misty and Elliot both were amazing singers. They didn't realize it, but their musical talent had come from their Dad, who was an amazing musician and singer as well. He would sing to them as babies, and they would listen to him singing until they both would go to sleep.

    Elliot was ready to leave, so he sent a text to her that it was probably time to go. Misty replied, "Wait just a few more minutes." So Elliot ordered another drink while he waited, and he sent another drink over to Misty, who was still at a table by herself. Misty had secretly put their names in to sing a duet together. After about five minutes of waiting, the karaoke host called up, "Misty and Elliot" and they were going to do "Endless Love."

    Elliot got up in amazement, and Misty followed him up there and the music started. They had never sung together before, but when they both started, they knew the singing range of the other. They blended with no problem. They sang their hearts out. They really knew the words, so instead of looking at the monitor for the words, they were looking at each other, and they even added a little bit of ad lib to the song. It was wonderful. After the song was finally completed, the whole bar was on its feet, and even the staff who worked at the club was clapping. After they sang, Elliot went to pay his bar tab, and the bartender told him that it was on the house. Elliot forgot that was one of their customs at the club. If you sang really well, they would give you a complimentary drink. So Elliot walked out first, and two minutes later Misty followed behind him. They still had to be careful as to who was watching them in the club. They both get into Elliot's car, and they drove off.

    Elliot drops Misty off at her car, which was parked at her friend's apartment. He kissed her and headed back to the ship.

    It was Wednesday, 9:30 a.m. It was a few days before Elliot was to ship out for two weeks. He got a call from Misty. Misty said she was sick. She told him that she has been throwing up all night and into the morning. She told him that she was on her way to sick call on the other side of the base. Elliot said okay but to keep him informed. He was really nervous and was wondering if she ate something that was bad. Then he started wondering if she was pregnant. He started getting nervous because amidst the fun they were having, they hadn't plan for anything like that.

It was 3:30 p.m., and Elliot still hadn't heard from Misty. Elliot was sitting at his desk on the ship, worried. He let his guys go early, so they could go and spend time with their families. At 5:00 p.m., Elliot's office phone rang and it was Misty. Misty said, "I have some news, honey."

He asked, "Are you okay?"

She said, "Yes, I'm okay, but I'm pregnant."

After hearing that, Elliot's stomach dropped, and he was in a state of confusion. He was scared and didn't know what to do. He told Misty that he had to see her that night. Misty said that she couldn't because she had to pull watch duty that night. It would have to be the next day. But that day just happened to be the day before the ships departure to the Caribbean for the two-week refresher trials. Elliot told her okay and asked if she could call him on his cell phone later in the evening. She said yes. He went to his rack in the officer's quarters and lay down to rest. He didn't feel so good. There in his rack, he was lying on his back, wondering what to do. He knew that he was in love with Misty, and he wanted to be with her, but he was also worried about his career. He wanted to return to football one day and become a football star. He fell asleep. Misty never called that night.

At 5:00 a.m., Elliot was so mentally drained. He had slept in his uniform. He got up and showers. He dressed and ran to his department where his guys were waiting in formation for the plan of the day. Elliot gave out the instructions and also the time to be back at the ship because they were pulling out the next day. He was going to let his crew off early to take care of their individual businesses, and he was going to meet Misty somewhere so they could talk.

At 9:30 a.m., he finally receives a call from Misty. Misty said that she was sorry for not calling but they were very busy on their watch last night. She said she had to see him today because she knew that the ship was pulling out in the morning. Elliot said that after afternoon muster, he would leave the ship and meet her at her friend's apartment, so they could go get dinner and talk. Misty agreed.

They met at the apartment. Elliot opened Misty's door, which he did all the time. She jumped in, and he got in and drove off.

For the first few moments in the car, no one was talking. It was completely silent. Then Misty asked, "What do you want me to do, Elliot?" He said, "What do you mean?" Misty told him that in no way, shape, or form was she having an abortion. Elliot agreed that he didn't ever want anything like that, but they had to figure out how to hide the fact that the baby was coming from a prohibited relationship that could land both of them in the basket. Misty kept telling him not to worry and that everything would be fine.

They continued to talk and talk and talk, and all of a sudden, Elliot broke out, saying, "Misty, I love you." She started to cry. She hesitated, and then she told him that she loved him too.

They have a really nice dinner together. Elliot had to drive about thirty miles away from Mayport to find a safe place to eat. They laughed and they talked. It was time for Elliot to get back to the ship. So they left, and he took Misty back to her car at her friend's apartment. They kissed, and they told each other that they loved one another then Elliot drove back to the ship.

Elliot had been out one month at sea. Their two weeks had turned into a month at sea because the captain decided that there was more training that needed to be completed before their six months' deployment that was about five months away. Elliot had only heard from Misty once, and it was through a letter. As the ship was pulling in, Elliot snuck a text to Misty, letting her know that they made it back safely. The ship finally docked, and Misty just happened to be at the ship side when Elliot got off. Of course, he wanted to hug her, but he couldn't due to the fact that they were both in uniform, and they didn't want their cover blown. She walked right by him, saluting him, and she winked as she saluted him. He saluted back with a wink as well. They ended up back at Misty's friend's apartment to hang out again.

Elliot told Misty that she looked really well, but instead of gaining weight, it looked as though she lost some. She told him that while he was gone, she lost the baby. She had to be rushed to the naval hospital, and they told her that she was no longer pregnant and that she had a complication that caused the fetus to abort.

Elliot was sad, and he knew that it hurt Misty. He told Misty that he loved her, and that one day, it will be done the right way. Elliot told her that God had a better plan. Misty told him that she qualified for an off-base apartment, and she would be moving in a couple of days. Elliot was excited for her.

It had been a week since Misty had been in her apartment, and she was loving the privacy. The apartment was about twelve miles away, and it was a good enough distance that whenever Elliot wanted to visit he should be able to do with no problem.

While sitting in her living room, Misty decided to call to Valdosta to talk with her cousin Alicia about Bruce's condition. Her cousin Alicia said he was still doing the same. Bruce was now in a nursing facility in Valdosta. He miraculously stayed alive despite the percentage of the damage done to his brain. He couldn't talk or move his limbs. He could only smile a little and bat his eyes.

Misty had put in a request to take a few days off to go and spend time with Bruce and to take care of more of his financial business. She would be leaving next Friday and returning back to Jacksonville on the following Wednesday.

Elliot called and said that he was on his way over to the apartment. She had to give him directions because Elliot hadn't been there before. He couldn't help her move because all of her enlisted friends were helping her. Elliot stopped at a department store, and he purchased a vase for Misty to put on her table or window. The vase was very expensive.

He finally arrived at the apartment after being turned around several times. He got out of his car with his housewarming gift and approached Misty's entrance. She opened the door and greeted him with a kiss, and she invited him in. They sat down on the couch and continued kissing. Elliot then handed her the beautiful vase that he purchased, and it made Misty so happy. She jumped up excitedly and placed it on her mantle. Misty informed Elliot that she had to go to Valdosta to check on her dad that weekend and that she would return on Wednesday. Elliot said that he wanted to go because he too had to go back to Macon to check on his parents as well. Elliot brought up the suggestion that they should go together. They could spend a day or two in Macon and then go back to Valdosta to spend the rest of the time with Bruce. Misty agreed. As she talked to Elliot, she went over to the stereo system, and she turned on some nice slow jazz. She went over to Elliot, and they started making love again on the couch. She was so happy that she finally had someone in her corner who truly loved her.

On Friday afternoon, Misty had just arrived at her apartment from the base. She had a very long day. She was already packed, and she went in to wait for Elliot. Elliot pulled up twenty minutes later, and they both packed their luggage in his car, and they were on the road to Macon first and then to Valdosta. While driving on the road, Elliot explained to Misty that he had been talking to his parents and Hazel about her and about them seeing each other. Misty was excited, but she asked, "Who is Hazel?" Elliot told her that she was the maid, but she was more of an aunt to him because she helped raise him. Misty asked, "Maid?" He said yes. Elliot never explained to Misty that he came from a very wealthy family and that they lived in a very large mansion. He never bragged about having money like that. He told Misty that his dad even bought the new BMW that they're riding in now as a graduation present from college. Misty was excited to see how her man grew up. She also couldn't wait to meet his parents and Hazel too. They were finally entering the subdivision where Elliot grew up, and Misty was amazed at the size of the houses there. Elliot turned in the circular driveway that passed right in front of the main door, and as usual, Hazel was the first one out of the house to greet the couple.

Hazel opened Misty's door, and Hazel immediately introduced herself and gave Misty a very big hug. Mr. and Mrs. Bennett came out of the house, and they rushed over to the car to finally meet Elliot's girlfriend. They introduced themselves, and then Jean hugged Misty. While Elliot was grabbing all the bags from the backseat, Steve walked over to him and said, "Son, she is beautiful. How did you meet her?" He explained blushingly that they met in Jacksonville. Jean took Misty inside, and she and Hazel started showing Misty around the house. They all were excited to meet their son's first serious girlfriend.

Steve explained to Elliot that, of course, they would not be sleeping together in their house, unmarried, so he told him that she would be sleeping in the guestroom downstairs.

After the long tour of the house and the grounds, Hazel informed everyone to have a seat at the table because dinner would be served in a few minutes. So everyone proceeded to the dinner table. Steve sat at the head, Jean at the opposite end and Misty and Elliot sat across from each other. Misty was just smiling and agreeing. She was so amazed at the size of this house and all the money that her man had. She was amazed that they even had a maid.

They had a very large dinner. Misty explained that she'd never been in an environment like that and that the house was the most beautiful she'd ever seen. She also told the family how beautiful they were. As they were eating, Steve turned to Misty and asked about her upbringing in Valdosta. He wanted to know about her family, her social status, and her hobbies. Steve asked her about her future plans. Misty explained that her family didn't have a lot of money. She explained that her dad did the best he could because he was a single dad. Misty started tearing up as she was talking. She explained that her mom and twin brother were killed when she was a baby. Jean asked her "My god, baby! How did it happen?" Misty explained that her mother and twin brother were on their way to visit family while she stayed behind with her dad, and they were involved in a bus accident. Steve got really quiet and asked, "Where did this happen?" Misty told him that from the stories she heard, it happened on I-75 in Florida, not too far from Valdosta.

Steve and Jean both got really quiet, and Steve almost choked on a forkful of corn that he had just put in his mouth. Hazel pushed her chair back in disbelief. Elliot looked at his dad, making sure that he was okay. Steve, now stuttering, asked Misty, "When did this happen?" She said that she was just a few months old, so it had to be in late 1982.

Immediately, Steve excused himself from the table and said that he had to go to his office for something. Jean followed right behind him. Hazel stayed at the table to continue entertaining Misty. On the way to his office, Steve was thinking, This can't be!

Misty and Elliot both didn't understand why both Steve and Jean abruptly left the table and ran to the office. Misty was scared she said something bad or hurtful. Elliot was giving all types of excuses of why they left, but he didn't know what was said either. Elliot excused himself from the table, and he ran to his dad's office to find his parents holding each other. Elliot asked them what was wrong, and Steve looked to him and made up a story that he was sad about what happened to Misty and Jean was consoling him. That seemed to be very fishy to Elliot, considering the fact that he never saw his dad emotional and especially over a story like what he had just heard. Elliot said that he was going back to the table to be with Misty. Steve and Jean followed right behind.

Arriving back to the table, Steve apologized to Misty, saying that her story really got to him, and he just had to get some air. Misty apologized. She said, "Whatever it was that I said, I'm truly sorry, Mr. and Mrs. Bennett." Jean told her that she had nothing to be sorry for.

The Bennett's had a baby grand piano in one of the rooms of their mansion. Elliot took Misty into the piano room. Elliot sat down at the piano and started to play. He was a gifted piano player as well as a singer, and while he played, Misty sang along with him. Steve and Jean walked in the room as the couple played and sang together, and they watched in amazement. Steve and Jean listened to that beautiful harmony that they both displayed, and they sounded so connected, Steve was thinking.

Steve went back down to his office while Jean stayed up with the couple. Steve was at his desk and he started looking through old news clippings that he kept from that horrible tragic bus accident back in 1982 when they found that little baby who was named Mitchell at the time. He saw some news clippings from a Valdosta news article saying that a baby was missing from the accident that had happened in Florida. The article had stated that there were no survivors from that accident...48 people were killed. He read the article of a man named Bruce Wilson who had lost his wife in the accident and they couldn't find his infant son Mitchell who just happened to be a twin.

Steve jumped up from his desk and went to his alcohol stash. He poured a half a glass of whiskey and drank it like water. He kept saying to himself, What have I done? Oh my god, what have I done?

Steve went back to the piano room where the lovely couple continued to play and sing, and he informed everyone that he was going to retire to his room. Jean said that she was going to turn in as well.

After an hour of playing and singing, Hazel showed Misty to her room, and Elliot headed up to his room. Misty was amazed at the size of the guestroom. She even had her own bathroom. She was in heaven, or so she thought.

Steve and Jean were both lying there in bed, but neither was sleeping. They both were thinking about the fact that this girl Misty could in fact be a twin of their son Elliot. They looked at each other while lying there. Jean had tears flowing down her face. She told Steve that they had made a horrible mistake, and it had come back to haunt them for what they did.

Steve and Jean woke to the smell of bacon and eggs that Hazel was preparing downstairs. Steve told Jean that they had to have a family discussion when the kids left that afternoon. She agreed.

Elliot met Misty downstairs in the living room, and they just kissed and hugged each other. Elliot asked how her night was, and she replied that she felt so relaxed in that room. That bed was amazing. They all gathered at the table for a good, hearty breakfast. Steve informed everyone that he had to go into the office for a few hours, but he would be back before the kids left for Valdosta.

After breakfast, Elliot decided to take Misty for a walk around the grounds of the house. Misty was amazed at all the trees, the beautiful flowers, and the beautiful pond that was about one hundred yards from the house. They sat on a rock by the pond, and Elliot said that he was glad and blessed that she was a very big part of his life now. He said that his plans were to finish up his military commitment and join the NFL. He also told Misty he wanted her to be with him. He admitted that he never felt that way about anyone, and that they had a connection that was so unexplainable. Misty agreed.

Misty told him that she had two more years of enlistment, and she wanted to get out and be with him.

Misty said she wanted a family, and she wanted to live together like Elliot's parents. She wanted to be happy, and she said that she felt that nothing or no one could ever come between them. Elliot agreed. Once again, they kissed very passionately, and they made their way back to the house.

When they arrived back at the house, Elliot went upstairs to his room to gather some more items to take back to the ship. Jean and Misty went into the living room and talked a bit about life there in Macon. Jean asked her what her intentions were with regard to Elliot. She wanted to know if there were plans of marriage in the future, and Misty replied, "I hope so." Misty said that Elliot has been the best thing in her life at that point, and she would love to be a good wife to him. Jean just looked very stunned when Misty replied with her answer. Jean said, "Okay." Jean also said that there were a lot of girls who wanted to marry Elliot. Then she looked with a cold stare in Misty's eyes and said in a low voice, "What makes you the one?"

Misty replied, "'Cause we have so much in common, and I love him for him and not what he has." Jean couldn't make a reply. She just sighed and went over and held Misty's hand. Elliot overheard them talking as he made his way downstairs, and he questioned Jean about why she was asking Misty about marriage and their future. Jean replied, "I was just curious." As they were talking, Steve pulled up outside, and Hazel immediately went to open the front door.

Little did they know, but Steve went privately to his office to pull up more information about the bus accident. Steve knew that he had done a horrible thing by taking the baby back to Macon, and at that point, he would just have to ride out the outcome of the decision he made. There was no way he was going to be able to tell Elliot the truth even if it meant that he allow them to marry, if that were to be the case. The only tactic that he could come up with would be to talk Elliot out of getting any closer to Misty. Steve didn't know that they had already tried to conceive a baby.

Elliot went out first to put some bags in his car, and Steve jumped out of his car and approached Elliot. He told Elliot that

Misty was a very pretty girl. He also told Elliot, "She's a very sweet girl, but I don't think she's the one for you, son." Elliot wanted to know why, and Steve said, "It's just a parent's intuition. She's not the one for you, son."

Elliot then questioned him about the night before, and how they all really liked Misty at first, and now the tables have suddenly turned. Elliot said that he was confused, but he had to get his girlfriend to Valdosta to check on her dad. He told Steve that they would talk later.

He walked over to the front door to get Misty's bag, and he told Misty, "We gotta go, hon." Elliot kissed his mother, kissed Hazel, and went to his dad and shook his hand. He and Misty walked to the car to get in. Before they could pull off, Hazel ran over to his car door and slipped him her cell phone number and told him that if he ever needed anything, he could call her anytime. They pulled out of the driveway and they headed to Valdosta.

All of a sudden, the Bennett household was in an uproar. Hazel ran upstairs, and she had all of her bags packed. There were two cars coming into the drive. They were family members of Hazel. Hazel told Steve and Jean that she quit because she didn't want to be a part of the lie that was taking place. She said that she also helped raise Elliot, and she had been following the story all along. She knew about his family in Valdosta, but she didn't know about his fraternal twin sister, and to top that, she didn't know that he was actually dating and had fallen in love with his twin sister. Hazel said that it was nasty and unethical, and she didn't want to be a part of this. Hazel also told Steve, "How can you sit back and let this happen to this sweet boy? You are a horrible, no-good, dirty bastard." She looked over at Jean and said, "If you allow this, then you're no better than him."

Jean ran upstairs, crying, and Steve couldn't believe what he was hearing. Hazel stormed out of the house and left after twenty-five years of being under the Bennett household. Steve put his head down. He slammed the door and ran upstairs to check on Jean.

Elliot and Misty had reached Valdosta, and Misty decided to go check on Bruce's house. She and Elliot went in. Alicia and Erica were there, cleaning. They were taking good care of the house. The two were so close that if you saw one, then the other was not far away. They were happy to see each other. Elliot hugged them both, and he noticed a picture that was on the bookcase. It was of Misty and her twin brother. He said that they were cute babies. Again, he didn't realize that he was in that picture as well. Misty grabbed some items, and they got back in the car to go over to the nursing home.

Arriving into Bruce's room, Bruce once again stared at Elliot. He got very agitated. Elliot thought that Bruce was just excited about seeing him, but in actuality, Bruce knew that Elliot could be his son. Misty ran over and kissed her dad, and they sat with him for several hours.

They decided to stay at the hotel for their stay there in Valdosta. While lying there in bed, Elliot started talking to Misty about what happened that day as they were leaving his house in Macon. He told Misty that he didn't know what got into his parents, and he couldn't understand why they were acting so strange. He apologized for their behavior and said that he would get to the bottom of it. Misty told him that they were sweet people, and they were just looking out for his welfare. She made a joke saying, "If my son looks as good as you do, I will do the same thang." They both laughed. They lay down and went to sleep.

They were able to spend a few days with Bruce, and they made it back to Jacksonville. The nurse told Misty that her dad was hanging in there, and he was a breathing miracle.

Elliot was preparing for that long six-month med cruise. Elliot often called his parents back in Macon, and they continued to try to discourage his relationship with Misty. Steve and Jean never told him that Hazel had quit and walked out of the house. Elliot and Misty had been spending every day together in some way or another. They continued to dodge all the military personnel to avoid getting busted for fraternizing. Though they were almost caught a couple of times by a few of the brass military officers at a restaurant.

There was only a few days left before Elliot is to leave out for six months. He arranged a very nice dinner at a very upscale restaurant in Jacksonville. They got really dressed up and made their way to the restaurant. Elliot had gone over to the restaurant earlier in the week to plan a special dinner for Misty.

When they arrived, the host sat them at a table that was located directly in the middle of the restaurant. The table sat all by itself and was draped with flowers, and it was really beautiful. There were a lot of people just staring at them. The people knew what was about to happen, but Misty didn't. Some of the kitchen personnel rolled the piano over to the table, and suddenly, the lights went down a little. Misty was really getting excited about what was going on. Elliot jumped up from his seat and sat at the piano, and there was a microphone at the piano. He simply said, "This is for my baby." He started to play a song by Larry Graham, "When We Get Married," but he sang it in his own way. He started singing, and Misty was crying along with all the other patrons and employees. He tore the song up. After he stopped, everyone started clapping. He got up from the piano and walked over to Misty and got on one knee. He simply asked, "Will you marry me?" He slipped a beautiful diamond ring on her finger. She immediately said, "Yes, honey. Yes!" He got up, and they kissed. They ate a wonderful dinner as everyone cheered them on. They finished their dinner and returned to Misty's apartment.

The couple sat on the couch, listening to some soft jazz, and they started to plan how they were going to get married without getting in trouble with the military. Elliot said that he wanted to get married as soon as he got back from the six-month cruise. He said he had already talked with navy personnel about trying to leave the navy early because there were some NFL teams that were still interested in him. Misty wanted a very small ceremony, and she was just ready to be Elliot's wife. She was getting frustrated with having to hide every time they went out to dinner or to a movie. She wanted a normal life with her husband-to-be.

It was the day before Elliot was to board the ship for the six-month cruise. Elliot parked his car at the storage facility, and he made sure that Misty was okay with money. They were spending as much time together as possible. She was going to drop him off at the ship later in the afternoon. As they were having lunch at a restaurant down at the Jacksonville Landing, they held hands and came up with suggestions for their future. Misty didn't want to stay in the military. She had another two years to go on her enlistment, but Elliot could get out next year after he got back from his cruise.

At 5:00 p.m., Misty drove Elliot to the ship. They realized they were taking a big risk by her dropping Elliot off like that. They didn't care at that point due to the fact they weren't going to see each other for another half of the year. She pulled directly on the side of the pier where the ship was docked. Elliot got out and walked around to Misty's door. He kissed her on the cheek, and he told her that he loved her and that he would be back in one piece. She said she loved him as well and then she watched him walk on the ramp and finally into the large aircraft carrier. She drove off crying and feeling lonely. Elliot was gone for six months.

It was the day before Elliot's return to Mayport. It had been a very long but successful cruise, and Elliot learned a lot. He had seen several countries. He received tons of letters from Misty. He sadly knew that Bruce had passed while he was out at sea and that Misty ended up selling the house to her cousins. His parents finally told him through a letter that Hazel quit and walked out on them, but they never said why. His parents also kept badgering him about finding a new girlfriend and trying to belittle Misty. There was one thing Misty said to him in a letter that had him on edge. She said she had a surprise for him when he returned. She refused to tell him what it was, and it drove Elliot crazy because he couldn't figure it out. Elliot did tell her through a letter that he found out that he may be released early from military service so that he could go into the NFL. The Detroit Lions and the New Orleans Saints were seriously interested in him playing for them.

There was a few hours left before the ship pulled into the port. All the sailors were standing along the side of the ship at parade rest. Elliot couldn't wait to get off and see his Misty. She somehow managed to get off of her duty to spend time with Elliot that day. The ship docked. They called for a mandatory muster for all the departments for the debriefing, and then they were released to disembark the ship. Elliot got off with the first group, and he was walking through the crowd to find Misty. She said that she would be in civilian clothes standing at the back of crowd by the fence. Elliot walked and walked. His cell phone was dead because he forgot to charge it. Finally, he found his Misty. He looks twice. She's big. His jaw dropped. Misty was seven months pregnant. He ran and hugged her, and they immediately left for the car. She was so happy to see him. He asked why she didn't tell him, and she said that she didn't want to distract him in any way. He was really excited.

They arrived at Misty's apartment, and they just embraced each other. He said that he was so sorry that he wasn't there for her at Bruce's funeral. She said that she understood. He told her that he was ready to get married. He said that he was going to take care of his family and that he didn't care about what the military thought anymore. Misty said that was fine, but she was more concerned with his career.

They talked about the baby, and Misty's pregnancy. He was so concerned about her health considering the last miscarriage she had. Misty explained that everything was going to be fine and she was taking her prenatal meds and not stressing about anything.

It's now Misty's ninth month, and Misty and Elliot were down at the justice of the peace. They got married. Misty's new name was Misty Marie Bennett. They both couldn't be any happier. They left and went back to the apartment.

Elliot wasn't going to file any paperwork stating that he was married just yet. He had a few more months before the Navy was to release him early. He was supposed to report to the Detroit Lions training camp in Lakeland Florida in about four months.

Elliot had been staying with Misty at her apartment. The ship wasn't going anywhere for a while. He'd report at 5:00 a.m. at the ship, and he would be home by 4:00 p.m. unless he had watch duty.

One morning, at 3:30 a.m. Misty jumped up screaming. Her belly was really hurting. Her water broke, and it was time for the little baby's arrival. Elliot drove her to the naval hospital, and he took her in. They didn't know that he was an officer. They got Misty up to labor and delivery. Elliot stayed out in the waiting area. He could hear Misty screaming at the top of her lungs. He couldn't take it anymore. He asked the nurse if he could he go in there with his wife. So they let him in, and he was holding Misty's hand while she was going through that horrible pain. The doctor called for an emergency C-section. So Elliot had to leave quickly and the surgical staff took over.

It had been three hours, and finally, the corpsman came out and asked Elliot if he was he any kin to Misty. He said, "Yes, I am. I'm her husband." The corpsman said that the nurse wanted to talk with him. So Elliot made his way to the nurse's office. Two of the naval doctors and a naval nurse started talking to Elliot about the baby. They told him that it was a little boy, but he had some serious health issues. He was deformed, and he had cerebral palsy. Elliot was stunned, and he didn't know why. The doctor's said that this was quite rare, and they eventually wanted to do more testing on Misty, and possibly some testing on him as well. Elliot told them that he needed them to do whatever it takes to help his son and his wife Misty.

Elliot scrubbed up and went into the room where Misty was recovering. She lay there, trying to wake up, and all she kept trying to say is, "Where's my baby?" The baby wasn't in the room yet. They were working on him in another room. After about twenty minutes, they brought the little baby in. His little face looked to be a little droopy. Other than that, he appeared normal. Misty was fully awake now, and they put the baby in her arms. She said that she wanted to name him Bruce Mitchell Bennett after her dad and brother. Elliot said, "Yes, that is his name."

The navy had given Misty maternity leave. So she was at her apartment, and Elliot was doing the fatherly duties. Little Bruce didn't cry a whole lot. He had a funny-shaped head and his face was droopy, but it didn't matter to Elliot because that was his son, and he went out of his way to take care of him and Misty.

Elliot's family was not thrilled about the birth of Bruce at all. At first, they refused to come and see the little guy. Elliot didn't understand why they didn't want to come and see their only grandson.

They sounded scared every time Elliot talked about the baby, but Steve told Elliot that they would make plans to come and see him soon.

The doctor's wanted Misty and the baby to come back to the hospital for some more labs in a few weeks. They told her that this was very interesting case because the baby should have been born healthy, but they wanted to figure out what went wrong. They did run prior tests when they were at the hospital, but they didn't show anything that would have suggested a major problem during the pregnancy.

Misty reported back to the hospital two weeks later. The doctor's started running more tests and lab work on her and the baby. Little Bruce appeared to be normal, but he just didn't cry. He would just look at you, and he would be slobbering heavily around the mouth. One of little Bruce's legs was longer than the other. It was becoming more significant as he grew.

Nine months had gone by so fast. Elliot had finally received his honorable discharge from the navy, and he was getting ready to head off to Lakeland Florida to workout with the Detroit Lions. He was so happy that he didn't have to hide from other naval personnel because his wife was enlisted. He was a little nervous about playing football again because it had been so long. He was the best when he played. He still held several records in the state of Georgia for rushing yards per game in high school football. He also still held records at the Naval Academy. He also knew that him having a degree in accounting, if his football career didn't happen, he always had his degree to fall back on.

Misty on the other hand had another year on her enlistment. The navy allowed her extra leave due to the fact that she was a mother of a special needs child, and they assumed that she was still single.

At nine months, little Bruce was still not crawling, and he still wasn't crying like a normal baby should. He wasn't playing like a normal child should be at his age.

It was time for Elliot to head off to camp, and he was to be gone for about three weeks. The doctor's had been telling him to come in for some testing, and he never went. So finally, on one of the baby's appointments, he and Misty both decided to go and see the physician who was asking for the labs.

They arrive at the office with little Bruce, and the doctor explains that he wanted to take four tubes of blood. He also wanted to take a swab sample from the mouths of Elliot, Misty, and the baby. He also wanted a complete family history from each of them. Elliot told him that he was adopted, and that he didn't know of his paternal parents or their medical history. The doctor asked if he still had his adoption paperwork, and if he did, he wanted him to bring it in.

There was so much paperwork to fill out, and the four tubes of blood turned out to be six. The doctor had the corpsman draw all the blood from each individual. The baby's blood work was very difficult to get, but the doctor had everything he needed. Elliot told him that he had recently been discharged from the navy and that he was headed to a football camp in Lakeland. The doctor said that it was no problem because it would be several weeks before he got the results back from all the testing, and still they would have to put everything together to come up with a reason why this little baby boy was not born healthy like he should have been.

Elliot didn't understand the fact that family history was very important to know before raising a family. It's good to know your medical history. He didn't think he had any diseases or anything and he didn't have high blood pressure, allergies, or diabetes. The doctor explained that this information was good, but they had to get more in depth with other things.

As they were talking with the doctor, Misty felt the same. She knew that she was healthy and didn't have anything physically wrong with her. Her dad died of complications of a stroke, but he didn't have any medical issues that she knew of. She explained to the doctor that her mom and brother died in a horrible accident, but she couldn't recall if she heard of her mom ever having any medical issues.

After the meeting with the doctor, the Bennett family decides to go to dinner and spend some family time together. Elliot was leaving in the morning for three weeks. He just wanted to spend time with his family and not worry about stuff he knew that couldn't change.

They ended up at a very nice steak house there in Jacksonville. Elliot grabs Bruce, who still isn't trying to walk or even crawl. They put him in a seat at the table. It was sometimes very hard to take him out to restaurants because he couldn't do anything at all for himself. He would shout out these loud bursts. He was close to a year old now. They understood that he was slow, and his legs were uneven. It just got very frustrating at times to Misty and Elliot. People would pass by and give him funny looks because of his droopy face. Misty hadn't even taken him to Valdosta yet, and neither had Elliot's parents been to see the baby. It was almost a year since his birth.

Elliot was getting ready to drive to Lakeland for his football camp. It was 7:00 a.m., and he put his bags in the car. He went back into the apartment and went over to where Bruce was sleeping. Elliot started to sing a song to him, something that he made up at the top of his head. Misty was there, drinking her coffee, and she tried to add words herself. Elliot arranged for a caretaker to come and help Misty while he was away. He explained to Misty that he was going to run those guys over, so he could get a contract. He told Misty that once he got signed in, she would never have to worry about anything else. Sadly, she walked him to the door. Elliot was so mad at his parents that he didn't even tell them what was going on about him and his football tryouts in Lakeland. He didn't even tell them that he was discharged from the navy.

As he was walking toward the door he looked over at Bruce, and Bruce acted like he wanted to wave to his daddy, but he couldn't. That brought tears to Elliot's eyes, and he went back over to kiss his son. Misty got up from her chair and ran over, and they had a big family hug for a few moments. Elliot had to leave. He left the BMW with Misty, and he took Misty's car. He wanted his family to be in style and safe while he was gone.

Elliot called as he arrived in Lakeland. He told Misty that he loved her, and that he couldn't wait till he got back home. Misty put the phone up to Bruce's ear, and Bruce tried his best to smile because he knew his daddy's voice. Misty told him not worry about anything and for him to do his best. She said that if he made the Lion's team, though she didn't want to live in Detroit because of the cold weather, but she would follow him to the ends of the Earth because she wanted to support her husband.

Elliot really showed that he still retained all that talent he had as a football player. He fit right in. He knew several of the plays that the Lion's offensive staff was calling in. He even played other positions, showing the Lions staff that he was very versatile in several positions. He fit right in with the team as well. A few team members were his teammates at the Naval Academy and even at Southwest High in Macon. The coaching staff was really impressed with his work ethics and how he took so much pride in every run. All Elliot thought about was his family every time he touched the ball.

The Lion's coaching staff was really impressed. They couldn't wait to see what Elliot could do in the preseason games that were coming up. There was another camp that was coming up, and that one would be held in Michigan. They wanted Elliot to attend, and the camp was for another three weeks.

During the time that Elliot was at the football camp, Misty was so busy taking care of Bruce. It was almost time for her to report back to duty on the base. She had been off close to a year. Little did she know, but the navy was preparing to discharge her because of Bruce and his special needs. The military still had her down as a single mother, and they were going to give her a general discharge that would turn to honorable in six months.

The doctor from the naval hospital called Misty at home. He asked her to come in because he wanted to get her and Elliot's fingerprint. She informed the doctor that Elliot was away and wouldn't be back for a couple of weeks. The doctor said, "That's fine, but I still want you to come in."

She went to the hospital, leaving Bruce at home with a friend from the base. The doctor pulls up some results from some testing that they took of her and Elliot. He said that there was something not right about their DNA, and that both of them were so similar by their tests results. Misty told the doctor that she was confused, and the doctor told her that he was confused as well. He needed Elliot for some more tests. The doctor took Misty's fingerprints and another blood sample, and then she was allowed to leave.

Misty got home and she made a phone call to Elliot's parents. She hadn't talked to them since they left Macon when she met them. They really were rude to her, so she didn't really have anything to do with them.

The phone rang, and finally, Jean picked up the phone. Misty said, "Hi, it's Misty."

Jean replied, "Hi, and how is Bruce?"

Misty said in a mean voice, "Bruce is fine. Now do you have some info on Elliot's medical history?"

Jean said no. Misty explained to her that the doctors have been constantly calling them into the office to do blood work, and she wanted to know why. She told Jean, "There could be something seriously wrong with Elliot, and you both don't act like you care."

Jean said, "I don't know what you're talking about." Steve was nearby, listening to the loud tone of Jean's voice. He grabbed the phone and told Misty that she was out of line, and she needed to calm down. Misty told him that they were wrong in how they had been treating them and also how wrong they were for not even coming to see their grandson. Misty got so mad that she hung up the phone while Steve was talking to her. Steve tried to call back, but Misty wouldn't answer his call.

Elliot finally pulled up at the apartment. He got out and got his bags and opened the door to find that Misty had prepared a big meal for him. Bruce was sitting in his specially made chair with a half-smile on his face. He was happy to see his daddy. Elliot dropped his bags and grabbed Misty and held her in the air. He kissed her, and then he ran over to his son and tickled him and kissed him on the forehead.

Elliot explained to Misty that the football camp went well, and the coaching staff really loved him. He had to return in a few days to Michigan for another three-week camp, and that one would be a little bit more intense. He also told Misty to not worry about bills. He had a nice savings account that Steve and Jean had set up for him when he was a baby. It was actually for college, but since he had so many scholarships, his college money in the account was for him to spend. He was really excited, and he explained that the Lions were offering his high school and college number to him as well. Good old number 5. Elliot was so excited.

Misty told him that the navy personnel office was putting through her paperwork for an early discharge. She was able to qualify because of Bruce's condition and as she was a single mother. They still didn't realize that she was married. She told him that the doctors wanted him to go back to the hospital for one more lab that they had to take.

Elliot got a little furious about why they wanted him to take another test. He said loudly, "There is nothing wrong with me! Why do they need another test?" Under his breath, he said, "Forget them." Then they sat down at the table to eat their big dinner. Misty had to feed Bruce as they ate.

Misty told Elliot after they ate that she called his parents and that she hung up on Steve. Elliot knew that his parents didn't like Misty for some strange reason. He asked Misty why she called them. Misty said she was just being honest, but she thought that Steve and Jean were hiding something from Elliot. She said that it was really strange that he had to go back for all those medical tests, and it appeared that Steve and Jean didn't even care. They hadn't even been down to Jacksonville to see their grandson. Misty just felt that it was very strange.

Misty insisted that Elliot go and give the doctor that last blood sample and his fingerprints. She said she was sick of it, and she wanted to know what was going on down there at that doctor's office.

The next day, Elliot went bright and early to the naval hospital to give the samples that the doctor needed for their very strange case. Elliot questioned why he had to give all these samples, and the doctor explained that they were finishing up on some testing and that he would have results very soon. Elliot asked him if he had some type of life-threatening disease or something. The doctor told him no and to stop worrying about it. It was just routine testing whenever they have an unnoticed complicated pregnancy such as what Misty had. After Elliot gave his sample, he left the hospital.

He spent the day with his family. They went to the beach. Little Bruce loved the ocean. He would perk up whenever he heard the ocean. Almost a year old now, and he couldn't play in the water like the other children because of his condition. They had a really good time.

It was now time for Elliot to go to the airport. Misty was going to drop him off. Misty's friend from the base was going to watch Bruce while Misty dropped off Elliot.

Elliot kissed Bruce and told him that he loved him and Bruce tries to say, "Bye-bye, Da." Elliot sheds a tear because he wants his son to be healthy and happy. Elliot told Bruce that he was going to try his best at football so that he can have a good life and be happy. Bruce, not understanding a word he said just smiled because he loved his daddy's voice.

Finally, Misty and Elliot were off to the airport. Elliot told her that he was going to try his best and that he loved her and Bruce. Elliot promised to get them out of that apartment and into a big house. She finally reached the airport, and Elliot jumped out with his bag. He ran over to the driver's side window and kissed Misty and told her that he loved her. He then went inside to check in. Misty pulled off in tears as usual.

It had been two weeks, and camp had been really going well for Elliot. He continued to impress the Detroit Lion's staff with his athletic ability on the football field. He was to play in the first preseason football game versus the Chicago Bears in a week. He was to start in that game.

Back at Elliot's hotel room, he and his roommate were sitting around, cracking jokes. They ordered a pizza and watched television. It was around 8:00 p.m. They did have a curfew of 10:00 p.m. The pizza arrived, and it was Elliot's turn to pay for the pizza because his roommate paid for the last one. He reached in his wallet. He needed twenty dollars. He didn't have a twenty, but then he remembered that he had a "just in case" money stashed away in a small pocket in his wallet. He pulls out a twenty dollar bill, and all of a sudden, a paper with a phone number popped out. It was Hazel's telephone number. Actually, it was her cell number.

He put the twenty dollar bill on top of the television in the room. He took Hazel's phone number and put it back in his wallet. He lay back on his bed and thought about Hazel. He hadn't talked to her in a very long time. They were very close as Elliot was growing up. Hazel had a big hand in Elliot's upbringing. He really missed her. It was Hazel who talked to him about sex and how to fight. It wasn't Steve. Hazel was the one who took him shopping. She wasn't just the maid, but she was more like the big sister to him in his upbringing. Elliot really respected her. Elliot wanted to call her, but it was really late. The pizza had just arrived, and they had to be up early for football drills in the morning.

The next day, Elliot once again proved that he was ready to be a professional football player. The coaches took him out of the practices and told him to save his energy because he was playing in next Thursday night's preseason game.

Elliot was so excited. He called home to Misty and told her the good news. Misty was so excited. She called her family in Valdosta and the few cousins she knew in Miami. She wanted them to watch the game next Thursday on television because Elliot was playing running back in the game. They were all excited, and they all said that they would watch the game.

It was Wednesday evening, the night before the first preseason Lion's game versus the Chicago Bears. The game would be played at Soldier Field in Chicago. The team was relaxing in their hotel rooms. They just finished a big team meeting and a humongous meal.

Elliot was walking along the hotel grounds, talking with Misty and he was telling her how excited he was about that football game. She told him that he should call his parents and let them know about the game. He decided to call them. He hung up from Misty and called his parents. Steve picked up the phone, and they talked. Steve said that he was sorry for the way he had been acting, but he was trying to protect his son from a mistake. Elliot asked, "A mistake from what?"

Steve told him to never mind that because he was married now and that he has a beautiful family to take care of. Elliot was still confused as to why Steve would say that, but he just ignored that statement from Steve and told Steve that he had been working out with the Detroit Lion's football team. He was to play in the first preseason game the next night. Steve was excited, and he called to Jean to come and talk with her son. She got on the phone with Elliot, and Elliot told her that he loved her and that he was sorry for not calling like he should have. She said that she was sorry as well, but she just wanted the best for her son. Again, Elliot had to let that statement go because it was apparent that they didn't care for Misty. Jean told her that she and Steve were planning on going to see Misty and the baby in a week or so. Elliot told them that they would have to talk to Misty and find out her schedule. Jean said that she would call her and get the details. Elliot told her to watch the football game on Thursday to watch him play. He said "Ma, I'm going to run over all of them."

She said, "Go, son. Do your thing. I love you more than you know."

Elliot got off the phone with them, and he decided to call Hazel. He let the phone ring and ring. He hung up before the voicemail came on. He was nervous to talk with Hazel. He hadn't talked with her in a very long time. He knew that she was going to get on his case about him not talking with her in so long. Elliot knew that they had a lot to talk about. He wanted to know why she quit so abruptly and just left his parents' house without a warning.

He called again, and this time Hazel picked up. She was so happy to hear from him. She asked, "What in the hell took you so long to call me?" He simply said that he thought he'd lost her phone number, and he had no other number to call and check on her. He told her that he was playing for the Detroit Lions and that his first preseason game will be televised the next night. She was excited, and she told him that she would be right in front of her television.

He told Hazel that he and Misty finally got married and that they have a son now named Bruce. Hazel was completely shocked, but she was happy at the same time.

Elliot then asked her why did she left and quit like that. She told him to never mind about that now. She wished that he would've called her earlier, and she would've explained why, but now it was irrelevant. She just wanted him to be happy with his family and to go and run those boys over and send her some tickets. She told him that she was always behind him throughout his football career and that she knew that he would make it.

She told him one thing that stuck on his mind. She said, "Sometimes we make mistakes unknowingly, but those mistakes can turn into the best thing that ever happened to you."

Elliot asked, "What does that mean?"

She said, "You'll see later in life."

Elliot told her that he loved her, and she said that she loved him too and would always be there for him. She also told him that he'd better not ever lose her number again. She wanted to see the baby as well. Elliot gave her Misty's number and then they got off the phone.

Elliot's game was starting in a few hours, and he called home to Misty and little Bruce to tell them that he loved them. She picked up the phone and said that a letter came to the house for them from the hospital. It said open immediately. Elliot said he wasn't in the mood for any crazy or bad news. He knew that the both of them were healthy, and he figured that the navy doctors were playing around with them. Elliot told Misty that he loved her and Bruce no matter what, and he wished Misty's discharge would speed up so they can move out of that apartment and further away from the stupid base. She agreed. She told him that she loved him, and little Bruce made some weird, happy noises because he knew daddy was on the phone. She said good luck, and they got off the phone.

Misty's curiosity got the best of her. She wanted to wait till Elliot got home to open the letter together, but there was no telling how long that would be now that he was starting the preseason football. She had several friends coming over to watch the game with her and Bruce in a few minutes, so she decided to wait and open the letter after the game that night.

Elliot did really well in his game. He ran over one hundred yards rushing, and the coach didn't even let him finish the game because he didn't want to risk Elliot getting hurt.

Everyone was impressed with his skills, and all of his family was calling Misty after the game, congratulating her on Elliot's game. Everyone in the apartment with her were cheering, drinking, and eating, and just having a good time. Even little Bruce was having a good time although he didn't understand what was going on.

It was late, and everyone had left the apartment. One of Misty's girlfriends, Mya, stayed and helped her clean up. Misty went into the room to put a chair back, and the letter from the doctor's office was on the bed. She finally opened it, and it said, "The tests are showing that the two parties, Misty Bennett and Elliot Bennett, are related in the matter of brother and sister. Probable twins. Most likely to be fraternal."

Misty fainted, and Mya heard her fall. Mya ran into the room and found Misty on the floor. Misty had hit her head on the bedpost. Mya called 911, and they responded quickly. Mya got little Bruce dressed, and they all went to the civilian hospital. Misty still had the letter in her hand. When the paramedics put her on the gurney, Mya grabbed the letter as they were taking her out. Mya read the letter and was in total shock. She had Misty's cell phone, and she called and left a message for Elliot. She told him that Misty had to be rushed to the hospital, and her name was Mya. She stated that she was a good friend of Misty's from the base clinic.

Elliot and the team were getting ready to board the bus and head to the airport. They were going to fly back to Michigan. His cell phone was dying. He saw that he had a message, and he waited until they got to the airport to listen to it.

He finally listened to the message, and he got very emotional. He didn't know what to do, so he called his father Steve. He asked his parents if they could drive to Jacksonville to see about Misty. He told him that she was rushed to the hospital there in Jacksonville. Elliot also called Alicia and Erica in Valdosta and told them what had happened. They said that they were on the way. Jacksonville was only about an hour and a half from their home.

Elliot was so worried as he flew back to Detroit. As soon as they landed, he tried using his friend's phone to call Misty's cell. He got no answer. He waited till they got to the hotel room and he tried again. After about five hours. He talked with Mya. Mya said that his parents showed up at the hospital, and that there were also other family members there that came from out of town. She explained that Misty had a small concussion, and she was going to have to stay at the hospital for a few days. She told him that his parents were going stay there as well. Mya gave the phone to Erica. Erica got on the phone and told Elliot not to worry. They were going to take little Bruce back to Valdosta with them. They knew how to take care of a special needs child. Elliot thanked them so much. He wanted to talk back to Mya.

Mya said that there was a letter that Misty was holding when she found her on the floor. Elliot said "What letter?" Mya said that he needed to read it for himself. Elliot pleaded with her to read it over the phone, but she said she couldn't and that she didn't want to be involved. She told him that she could give it to his parents, who were in the waiting room. Elliot told her loudly, "No no no! Don't give them anything."

She said, "Fine."

He told her that he would see if the coaches would let him fly home for at least the weekend for the emergency. So Mya gave him her number as well.

Elliot was able to get clearance from the coaching staff to go home and take care of his family business. He was to return on Monday evening before the team meeting. They had another preseason game the following Thursday.

Elliot arrived in Jacksonville the next day. His parents were there at the airport to pick him up. They were so happy to see each other. They took him back to the hospital. Misty still hadn't gotten discharged yet. Elliot's parents had no idea about the letter that came to the apartment with that information that caused Misty to collapse.

They arrived at the hospital, and Elliot ran up to her room. She was lying there, sedated, and Mya was there as well. Elliot kissed his wife on the head, and he told her that he loved her. She smiled at him, and she went right back to sleep.

The doctor came in, and she explained that she hit her head pretty bad. Misty had a concussion. The doctor wanted her to stay for a few days for observation. Several of the physicians on staff recognized his name by looking at Misty's charts. They knew he was an upcoming football player because they saw the Lions' game as well, so they were stopping by Misty's room, occasionally asking for an autograph or picture. Elliot didn't mind because he was humble like that.

Elliot's parents were in the room as well. Jean was sitting over by Misty, and Steve was standing by the door. They still had no clue about the letter in Mya's pocket.

Mya was scared to death about giving Elliot the letter because she knew that that letter could destroy him, his family, and his career. Mya wasn't sure what Elliot would do either. He might even kill himself.

Elliot was staring at his wife. He looked up at her IV bag and then looked at Mya and asked, "Where is that letter?" Mya hesitated and then said, "Let's go outside."

Elliot told his parents to watch Misty. He would be right back. Elliot and Mya walk toward the cafeteria, and she reached in her pocket for the letter that Misty received from the doctor's office to give to Elliot. As she did, Elliot received a very important call on his cell. So he told Mya, "Just a second." He walked off to get a little bit of privacy to talk. Mya reached in her pocket to pull out the letter anyway and figured out that it was not there. She made a mistake and put the ripped envelope in her pocket instead of the letter itself. The letter must be in her purse, which was in Misty's room.

Elliot gets off the phone, and he informed her that it was a call from his coach, and he had to make another call to his newly appointed agent. So he told Mya that he would meet her back upstairs in Misty's room. Mya said okay. She didn't mention that she didn't have the letter, and it appeared that Elliot forgot about it, or so she thought.

She went back at Misty's room to find that Misty was up, and Jean was rubbing her head. Misty smiled at Mya and thanked her for taking care of her. Steve and Jean also thanked Mya for what she had done for Misty.

Steve said that he was hungry, so he offered to take Mya with them for something to eat. Mya agreed because she said that her stomach was growling anyway. Mya walked over to Misty and told her that she would be back, and that Elliot was downstairs on a very important phone call from his coaches. Misty said, "Go, Mya. I'm sleepy anyway." Before Steve and Jean could get out of the door, Misty told them very softly, "Thank you for coming, but we gotta talk."

Jean said, "I know, baby, but get your rest. We'll be right back." They went to a restaurant across the street.

Elliot showed up in Misty's room about ten minutes later. He walked over to her and kissed her and asked, "Baby, what happened?"

Misty refused to tell him the truth, so she said that she tripped and fell.

Meanwhile, Steve, Jean, and Mya were sitting at the restaurant. They ordered their food and drinks. Steve said that he would pick up the check. Mya thanked Steve and Jean for the lunch. Mya asked if they knew about a letter that Misty was reading when she fainted. Steve told her no. Steve asked what letter was she referring to, and Mya replied, "Just a letter from the navy about her getting out of the service."

Mya didn't want to start any problems, so she lied to Elliot's parents. They were still not aware of the actual reason why Misty fainted. They continued lunch, and Steve and Jean got more acquainted with Mya. They finished lunch and returned to Misty's hospital room.

They returned to the room to find Elliot there sitting next to his wife. Steve told Elliot that it was time for him and his mom to head back to Macon because he was assisting in a case one of his partners at the firm was handling. Elliot walked over to his parents and said, "Thanks for coming down to see about Misty." He turned to Misty and told her that he was going to walk his parents down to the door. Misty said, "Okay, honey," very softly. Both parents walked over to Misty and kissed her on the forehead and then they left.

A few seconds after they left, Mya got up from her chair and ran over to Misty and asked her, "Misty, what the hell is going on? Is that letter true, hon? What are you going to do? That's nasty, girl. Is it true?"

Misty replied, "I do not have a clue, but you have to promise me that you cannot say anything to anyone. Steve and Jean don't even know what's going on, but they could be the cause to all of this. I'm going to get to the bottom of this because I cannot live my life like this."

Mya understood, and she told Misty that she would keep everything hush, hush. And if she needed her help, she would be there for her.

The nurse walked into the room and told Misty that she could be discharged in an hour or so. The nurse told her that all of her X-rays and lab results came back negative, so she was free to go home.

By that time, Elliot had returned to the room, and the nurse told him the same thing. The nurse was also a football fan, and she remembered Elliot from playing at the Naval Academy. She said, "It is such a pleasure to meet you." Elliot gave her an autograph, and she left.

Elliot was excited that his wife was finally able to go home. He and Mya both gathered Misty's things and got her dressed. The nurse came with the wheelchair, and they headed downstairs. While walking to the elevator, more people started staring at Elliot because they remembered his face from watching NFL preseason football games. His celebrity status was starting to kick in.

They finally made it to the car, and Mya helped Misty in the car while Elliot jumped in the backseat. As Mya drove back to Misty's apartment, Elliot informed her that he received a phone call while at the hospital. And since everything was okay with Misty now, he was going to take the late flight back to Detroit because he was going to meet with his agent in the morning about his contracts. He told Misty that the Lions was ready to sign him, and his agent was negotiating with the owners at that moment. He explained that the sooner he signed the papers, the sooner they could move into a big house.

Mya was excited for them. "Wow! That's wonderful!" she exclaimed rather loudly. Mya stated to Misty that she wished that she had a boyfriend or husband to do that for her. Misty laughed.

After hearing all of that, anyone hearing the news would've been excited to no end, but Misty's reaction was very bland. She would reply in a soft monotone, and she wasn't as boastful as usual. She was almost like a deer caught in the headlights.

They finally get to the apartment, and Mya had to head back to the base. Mya had to prepare for inspections the next day, so she had to go back and get her uniforms and get the barracks cleaned and ready. She told Elliot that it was nice meeting him and wished him good luck in his football. She also told him that she would be there for Misty, and she would check on her every day.

Elliot told her thank you and gave her $200 in cash. He said, "I know it's tough for an E4 out here, so take this money and buy yourself something nice." Elliot said that he was just showing his appreciation.

"Thank you so much. Now I can buy some shoes," Mya said, laughing. She left.

While in the apartment, Misty was still acting very shy and quiet. She went into the bedroom and turned on the television. Mya had given her the actual letter back, and Misty had put it back in her back pocket. Elliot came into the bedroom, and Misty said, "There it is. That's what I tripped on." It was one of her shoes that were by the bed. Elliot believed it. So he told her to lie down and do as the doctor ordered. Elliot told Misty he had to go to the pharmacy to pick up her medicine and take care of some other business. She said okay. He kissed her on the cheek and left.

When he left, she immediately called Erica to check on her baby. Erica answered and said that he was fine, and he was enjoying the family there in Valdosta. Misty said that he was going to have

Elliot wire some money to them to help with the expenses while she recovers.

Erica said, "No problem." She explained again that Bruce was having a good time interacting with the family and she and Alicia would take turns watching him. She told Misty that he was welcome to stay as long as she wanted him to. Misty was so relieved.

Misty pulled out that letter again, and she reread it over and over again. She couldn't believe what she was reading. She kept having crying spells, and her eyes were swollen. She started to go into denial mode. She kept chanting, "This is a freakin' joke, and there is no way!" She just kept on chanting this. She was thinking, What were the chances that she marries her dead twin brother? "No way! No way!" She started crying again loudly, "No way!" She picked up and threw a magazine it against the bathroom door while screaming. She lay down on the bed and fell asleep.

In about an hour, Elliot returned with Misty's meds. He had taken care of all his business. He had also picked up the mail from the box. He went through it and found a letter from the Department of the Navy. It was addressed to Misty. It was wrong, but he decided to open it anyway. To his surprise, it was her discharge paper. She was officially out through special permission. Elliot was so happy for her. In his mind, they could move on and live their lives free from the military, and that would be nothing tying them down.

He walked in the bedroom. Misty was in deep sleep. She had put the letter into her front right pocket. Elliot knew that he had to get to the airport to take that flight, so he tried to wake her up, but she was so out of it. He said, "Honey, I gotta get to the airport. I don't want to leave you, but I gotta go, so we can get this contract signed."

She said, "Go, hon. I'll be fine. I'll have Mya come back over tomorrow because I'm just going to sleep tonight."

Elliot hesitantly said, "Okay, baby. I put your medicine on the kitchen table and your mail is on the dresser. I got the oil changed on the car, and you have nothing to worry about."

She again said okay. Elliot told her that he had a cab on the way and that he was going to call when he arrived in Detroit later that night.

UNINTENTIONALLY CONNECTED

A few minutes later, Elliot heard the horn from the cab outside. He grabbed his bags and he yelled, "Honey, I love you!" He didn't hear anything from her, but he knew that she was still sleeping. Elliot walked out of the apartment and got in to the cab and headed for the airport.

On the way to the airport, he felt something was very odd with Misty. She didn't tell him that she loved him at all, and she wasn't talkative like she normally was. He figured it could be that she was just exhausted and/or just feeling the pain from that horrible fall. He knew that he just had to remain mentally focused on his football play because he knew that he had to get his family out of that apartment. He knew that Bruce was going to need extra care, so he wanted to make sure that his son was well taken care of.

He reached the airport, and he put his headphones on. To his surprise, as he was listening to an old-school radio station, the song that was playing was "When We Get Married" by Larry Graham. He was so happy. He walked to the waiting area to sit and wait for his gate to start letting passengers on. He just knew that all of it was meant to be, or so he thought.

The next day, Misty was feeling a little better. She immediately called the doctor's office to set up a time to go and talk with him about the lab results. The corpsman at the naval hospital told her to come in at 10:00 a.m. and then she could consult with the doctor. In the meantime, she lay on the bed in shock over the letter that she has back in her hand. She kept reading it over and over again and was still crying in disbelief. All she wanted were answers. She hasn't eaten anything, so she was very weak.

She made it to the hospital, and the corpsman took her information and then sent her to the back. She walked into the doctor's office, and he told her to have a seat. She sat and he said, "Hon, I know why you're here. You want answers, and you want me to give you a solution. I can't. How did this happen?"

Misty told him while crying, "I don't know how this sort of thing happened to us. To me! Why?"

The doctor told her that they had never seen a case like that, so they wanted to do some more investigation, but he couldn't. The doctor knew that she had just been recently discharged from the military, so the doctor had to recommend the case to a civilian social worker and doctor. He told Misty that that was the reason that the baby was born the way he was and that they couldn't have any more children if they preferred to stay together. He told her that she's in a very challenging predicament. "You have some very difficult decisions to make, Mrs. Bennett," he said.

Misty was looking at the floor, still in a daze as the doctor spoke to her. The doctor wrote all the information down, and he said that he had already made a call to the social worker to start to help Misty in that weird ordeal. The doctor said that he had another patient, and he wished her good luck in her endeavors and that if there was anything else he could do, to just let him know. He rose from his chair. Misty rose to her feet, and they shook hands. He slipped the information on the paper to her and then Misty walked out of the naval hospital for the last time.

Misty got in her car, and she headed back to the apartment. She figured that she'd call the social worker later that afternoon. She wasn't feeling up to talking about that issue at the time. She did call Mya on her cell phone to see if she could come by later in the day to talk and spend time with her. She had to leave a message due to the fact that Mya was still at work. Mya was also a dental tech, and she worked alongside Misty while she was still in the navy.

She returned to the apartment, and she just realized that she hadn't called Elliot back yet. He left her a message last night after he arrived in Detroit, and he told her not to call but to get her rest. It was already 3:00 p.m., and she still hadn't talked to him.

While in the apartment, Misty tried to eat something, but she couldn't. She tried to eat a bowl of cereal but immediately threw it back up. Her nerves were getting the best of her, so she just lay down to try and sleep. She realized that, technically, she was unemployed, and her only source of income now was through her husband/brother now. She started crying even more. She thought about her dad and how he thought that Mitchell was dead, but yet, he resurfaced as her husband. She thought back to when Bruce saw Elliot last and how he perked up whenever he was in the room. She cried herself to sleep.

Mya was ringing the doorbell, and Misty jumped awake and answered the door. Mya came in and hugged Misty. She asked if she was doing any better. Misty replied, "No." Mya also asked if she had talked with Elliot, and Misty said no.

They both sat at the dining table. Mya asked, "So are you going to divorce him on the basis that you both are brother and sister, let alone twins?"

Misty replied that she didn't know what to do. She told her that Elliot was the only love that she ever knew. That he was the very first sexual experience she'd ever had. "We have a child, for god's sake!" Misty said loudly. She started to cry very hard all over again. Mya got up and held her. Mya told her that she was going to have to get herself together before she had a nervous breakdown. Mya suggested that they come up with a plan of attack. She said, "Clearly, you and Elliot didn't have anything to do with this, but we have to find a solution."

Misty explained that she had to go talk with a social worker and a new doctor that the navy doctor had recommended her to. "I really don't want Elliot to know this yet. Let me come up with something first because I don't know what his reaction will be," Misty said. Mya understood. Mya said that she was going to go out and get something to drink. Misty said, "Fine."

It was late Friday afternoon, and Mya returned with some bottles of vodka and orange juice. Misty wasn't a heavy drinker and neither was Mya, but that night would change that. It was too late to call the social worker to set up some type of appointment, and Mya was off for the weekend, so they were going to chill that night.

Misty's phone started to ring, and she looked at the caller ID. It was Elliott. She didn't want to talk to him, so she just let it ring, and it went to voicemail. His message was that he hoped that she was feeling better and that he loved her. He wanted to inform her of the good news of his contract. He also said he would call back later.

Misty and Mya start drinking their booze and drinking heavily. Mya thought that Misty needed to be relaxed in her mind as much as possible, so that was the reason she went out to get the liquor for them. They would drink well into the night.

At 12:30 a.m. Misty was very drunk at that point. Mya was tipsy, but she gave the bulk of the liquor to Misty. Misty started yelling, "I can't ever touch him again. It's my freaking dead brother. I had my dead brother's baby. Why me? He just happened to be the only man I ever loved. He was my first!"

As Misty's screams turn into heavy crying, Mya was still trying to comprehend the fact that her dear friend, whom she really cared for, had married her fraternal twin brother and had a baby by him. Mya still couldn't believe it.

The two slept until 1:00 p.m. Saturday afternoon, and Misty woke to the sound of the phone. It was Elliot calling on the cell. She picked it up this time. "Hi, honey," she says. "How are you?" He said he was fine. He was concerned about why she wasn't picking up the phone last night. She told him that Mya came over and they drank last night. Elliot calmed down, and he told her that he had some good news about his contract. He was to sign for $1.3 million a year. He wanted to find out if little Bruce had returned home yet, and she told him, "Not till next week." Little Bruce was to stay two weeks with Alicia and Erica. Elliot asked Misty what were her plans for the day was, and she told him that she just wanted to relax and watch television. She was also getting ready to fix Mya and her something to eat.

Mya heard their phone conversation from the living room. She screamed, "What's up, big E?"

Elliot heard her and told Misty to tell her, "What up, kiddo."

Elliot felt the coldness from this phone call, and he decided to lie about why he had to get off the phone. He told Misty that the coaching staff called a meeting, so he had to get off the phone. He told Misty bye and that he loved her, and she said, "Ditto." She promised to talk to him later.

Elliot was starting to feel that something was not right at home. He felt that maybe Misty was having an affair because of her cold responses. He was reminiscing about their times at the club and of how she was so lively and funny, and all of a sudden, she was just cold with her responses and made no conversation anymore. Elliot knew something was going on.

The Detroit Lions had one more preseason football game. The Lions were playing the Pittsburg Steelers, and the coaching staff didn't want Elliot to play because he had proven himself. They didn't want him to get hurt. So they just primarily wanted him to take stats and just relax and watch the other up and coming football players. So Elliot asked his coach if he could he miss the last preseason game. The coach told him no. He had to be present. The coach explained that it would be the last cut, and it was disrespectful to the team if all team members were not present. Elliot agreed.

At Thursday afternoon, Elliot was getting ready to call Misty. He wanted to surprise her and tell her that he wanted her to look at a house there in Jacksonville Beach. He was going to purchase a house on the water for her and lil Bruce. They had gone riding one day, and they saw a house on the water that was for sale, and Misty had said that she wanted to buy one day. It was the same house that Elliot wanted her to go and look at because he was ready to purchase it.

He called, and she picked up. Elliot noticed that she didn't sound as down as she had the last few weeks. She told him that she is sorry for how she had been acting. She just needed some time to relax. She said she was just exhausted by all the changes that were going on and all the decisions that were taking place. She told Elliot to have a good game. She would see him soon. Elliot told her that he would be home on Saturday for a week before the season starts. He hung up then headed to the stadium to get suited up for the game.

Misty didn't mention to Elliot that she had been seeing a social worker and a psychologist. She told her story to them, and they were trying to come up with a solution to deal with the problem. The social worker turned the case over to the psychologist. Misty was really in need of some evaluation. She had been drinking heavily and was very depressed. Little Bruce was still in Valdosta with Alicia and Erica. She was not in any shape to care for him at that point.

The Lions eventually lost the game to the Steelers, and Elliot didn't really care because it was a preseason game. He called Misty after the game, and she said that she was sorry they lost. She said that she was going to see lil Bruce in Valdosta in the morning and that she would be spending the day in Valdosta with the family. She said that she would talk with him in the morning. She didn't tell Elliot that she was also driving to Macon to see his parents.

It was 11:00 a.m. Misty didn't call Steve and Jean to tell them that she was coming. She had so many questions for them because, at the back of her mind, she felt they had a lot to do with what was going on.

She remembered how to get to the big house, and she pulled up into the circular drive and turned the engine off. A slim middle-aged man came out of the house. He was the butler there now. He took Hazel's place. He opened the door and asked, "May I help you?" Misty said that she was there to see Jean and Steve. He said, "Wait just a second."

Jean was walking down the stairs, and she saw Misty at the door. She immediately yelled to Steve that they had company. Jean invited Misty in, and she and Jean went into the living room. Steve entered right behind them.

Misty said she knew what was going on. Jean and Steve both looked puzzled. Misty said, "I know what you both did now." Steve and Jean were still denying that they know anything. Misty says, "You kidnapped my brother. I know you did."

Steve finally came clean. He said, "Yes, Misty. Unfortunately, we did come up on that horrible accident. I stopped to see if I could help, but I couldn't, and all I heard was this little baby crying, and I knew I had to get over to save it. Jean stayed in the car while I did this. We actually were on our way to a vacation. Jean and I had been trying to get pregnant for a very long time, and I was not acting sinister, but I saw this as an opportunity to give this little baby a beautiful life. I never meant to hurt anyone, and I never would have suspected that he would run into a fraternal twin sister, fall in love, and then eventually marry her, and have a baby on top of all that. What were the odds of that? At the time, I was thinking that this little baby has just lost his mother and probably his whole family. I just wanted to give this baby the best life I could." He started crying as he was saying this. Jean is in tears and she lowers her head in her lap crying.

Misty started talking loudly and ended up yelling, "What you have done is that you have destroyed my family. You have caused us to commit incest unintentionally. You both have caused my dad to die without seeing his son whom he dearly loved." She got up and started walking toward the door still yelling and crying at the same time. "You have caused me to have a miscarriage, and now my son Bruce will never be like other kids. He will never have a normal life, let alone walk on his own. You both have destroyed us."

Steve got up and ran in front of Misty. He looked into Misty's eyes, and he said, "I'm truly sorry, Misty. I'll do anything to make that up. Money. I have lots of money. You will never have to work again. I'll have the best medical care for Bruce. I'll get you cars… whatever you want. I'm sorry. We're sorry. Misty, please know that our intentions were never to hurt you or anyone for that fact. Please, Misty. What can I or Jean do?"

Misty looked him in the eyes and very hesitantly she said in a very low, informative voice, "I'll tell you what y'all can do to solve this…. *Tell Elliot!*" Then she walked out the door.

Steve followed her, yelling, "I can't. I can't! He won't have anything to do with us if I did that! Please, Misty, don't do this! *Please!*"

Misty jumped in her car, and she drove off, burning rubber in the driveway.

The butler was in the kitchen, listening to all that. He was in shock. He was thinking now that he was working for two barbarians. Jean walked in the kitchen, and she looked at the butler, but he was putting up dishes and acting like he heard nothing.

Misty was now on her way to Valdosta to see her baby little Bruce. She's thinking that Bruce was the only innocent victim in that mess of a relationship and he would be paying the price with his life.

Misty arrived in Valdosta, and before she got to her old house, which now belonged to Alicia and Erica, she visited the gravesite of her mom and her dad. As she walked toward the graves, her eyes filled with water. She looked at the headstones and said, "Mommy and Daddy, what have I done?" Bruce's, Leatha's, and Mitchell's names were all inscribed on the tombstone. It's a family plot, and they all were to be buried there together. "What am I going to do? Please help me." She looks at Mitchell's name on the family tombstone, and she cried out very loudly, "I married you. You're not dead, Mitchell. You're Elliot. Why, why, why!" She fell to her knees and screamed, "I don't know what to do, Mama!"

She eventually got herself together and went to the house were Bruce was. It was her old house. Alicia and Erica took it over after Misty said that she didn't want it after her dad died.

When she got to the house, Alicia let her in. As Misty entered the house, she couldn't stop crying. Erica came from in the bedroom where little Bruce was sleeping, and both she and Alicia grabbed Misty and held her. They both asked, "What's wrong, baby?"

Misty told them to call all of the family over because she had a very big announcement to make. They were wondering what it was. Misty told them again to call all of the family over and to hurry. So Erica got on the phone and started calling all the family over. As Alicia and Erica were calling everyone, Misty went into the bedroom and lay next to Bruce as he slept. It would be three hours before everyone showed up. Erica went into the room, and she woke Misty up and told her that everyone was present and that they all were waiting for her to say what she had to say. Misty put Bruce in his chair, and she rolled him out into the living room. Everyone was glad to see her. They were actually smiling until she started to talk. Her cousin David, who happened to be the pastor at a church in Valdosta, was there.

She got everyone's attention and she said loudly, "My twin brother is not dead." Everyone got so quiet that one could hear a pin drop. She said, "I have just found out, and I have proof that my husband, Elliot, is my lost twin brother who was kidnapped at the bus accident, and here is the proof." The room got a little agitated, and some even ran to the porch, crying. They were startled and in shock. Misty started crying and shouting, "I don't know what to do. I don't know what to do." Everyone grabbed her, and they held her, crying. Her cousin, the pastor, said a big prayer. After the prayer,

Misty asked everyone not to tell Elliot but to let her handle it and to just pray for her.

Alicia bought some chicken, and some other family members brought food over. They all ate and comforted Misty. They entertained little Bruce. They would all leave in a few hours to return to their own homes. The pastor stayed behind to talk and counsel Misty. He told her basically that it was a case of incest, but it was not her fault. But she had to make the right decision to correct the sin that she was wrongfully involved in. Misty didn't reply. She just put her head down in sorrow.

She would head back to Jacksonville in the morning because Elliot was to return home before his first game that was to be played in Minnesota. Misty and Erica offered to keep Bruce, but Misty said no. She needed her baby with her.

Misty arrived back in Jacksonville, and she's thinking about what to do. How do I tell Elliot about this horrible situation? Elliot was on his way home for a few days. The NFL season was starting up. She and Bruce were in the apartment, and to her amazement, little Bruce couldn't talk, but when he heard a song on the radio that he liked, he tried to hum to the beat of the song. Misty thought it was so cute.

The phone was ringing, and Misty looked to see who it was. It was Elliot, calling from the airport in Detroit. He said he would arrive at 7:00 p.m., so Misty replied, "Okay, hon."

Misty had the letter in her hand from the doctor's office. She just couldn't put it down. The letter was starting to get very worn because she let her family read and reread it in Valdosta. She and Bruce lay down to take a long nap until Elliot had to be picked up at the airport.

Finally, Elliot had arrived, and Misty and Bruce were out in the parking lot, waiting for him. Elliot only had one bag because he was not able to stay long this time.

Elliot reached the car and he immediately opened the back door and kissed Bruce. Bruce was so excited to see his dad. Then Elliot jumped in the front seat and kissed Misty. He tried to intimately kiss her, but Misty refused him.

Elliot asked, "What's wrong with you, honey?" She said that she was just tired, and she was hungry. Elliot said, "Let's go get something to eat." He was so happy to be back at home with his family.

As they were driving to their favorite restaurant in downtown Jacksonville. Elliot started explaining that he had deposited $250,000 into their account. Misty replied, "That's a lot of money." Elliot said that it was just the beginning. He told her that their family was going to live really well from then on. He also told her that she could pick out any house that she wanted. He asked her if she got a chance to tour the house in Jacksonville Beach that they had admired before they got married. Misty told him that she hadn't had the chance to get there yet.

While at the restaurant, Bruce was having a good time. He loved being around his dad. He would just smile from ear to ear. Elliot noticed that Misty just appeared to be preoccupied. Elliot said, "Baby, what's wrong? You have been acting like this for some time now. Why are you treating me like this?" She said that there was nothing wrong. She was just tired, she replied. They finished their food and headed to the apartment.

In the apartment, Elliot was reading all of his mail that piled up. He started playing with Bruce on the couch. Misty was in the kitchen with the letter in her hand. She wanted to let him read it now, but she thought that it just was not the time for that. She thought that she should just play it off like nothing was going on for the meantime, and when the time was right, she would slip him that letter. She just didn't know how his reaction was going to be. She put it back into her pocket, and she joined the two out in the living room.

Finally, Bruce went to sleep on the couch beside Elliot. Misty was sitting on the floor just watching them. She wasn't sleepy at all. She stayed up through the night, thinking of what to do.

The next day, the family all went out looking at houses. Misty was in a little better mood. Again, little Bruce was just laughing and playing with his dad. They finally look at the house in Jacksonville Beach. The sales agent from the real estate office was giving them all the details of that big, beautiful home. Elliot told Misty that he could buy this house today if she wanted it. She said that she wanted to look at some more before making her decision. Elliot said okay. They looked at four more houses, and they were tired. Misty did say that she loved the house in Jacksonville Beach, but she didn't want to buy the first thing she saw. Elliot, being the gentleman, told her, "If that's the one you want then I'm going to make sure that my wife is satisfied." Misty smiled.

Elliot was to leave in the morning, and this time, he would be gone for two months due to the Detroit Lions' schedule.

They all went to dinner again, and this time, they went back to the restaurant where Elliot proposed and sang that wonderful song to Misty. As they ordered their food, Misty started to cry again. That caused little Bruce to start crying. Elliot couldn't figure out what was wrong. She just looked at Elliot and said that the night he sang to her was just so beautiful. She wished that that particular night would not have ever ended.

They have a wonderful dinner and then returned to the apartment. Elliot put Bruce to bed, and then he went into the bedroom with Misty. They talked about how to handle all of Elliot's bills while he was away, playing football. He made sure that Misty wouldn't want for anything. He had new insurance paperwork for her to sign, and he told her that every week, a new deposit would be going into the account. Misty said that she would take care of everything, and she would have everything organized while he was away.

It was late. Elliot reached for Misty and gently pulled her into his arms. He caressed her and started kissing her all over her body as he undressed her. Misty didn't want to, but she knew she had to. She opened her legs and just lay there as Elliot made love to her. Misty thought that if she just cooperated that one time, everything would be fine. She had hidden the letter from the doctor's office in Elliot's bag in one of the pockets along with a letter she wrote. They made love for a good long time, and Misty faked all the orgasms that he thought she was having. Then they lay there and slept until the morning.

It was 6:30 a.m. It was time for Elliot to get to the airport. Misty got Bruce ready, and they were off. When they reached the airport, Elliot leaned over and kissed Misty and told her that he loves her more than the world itself. She replied, "I love you too." Elliot got out and opened the rear door and kissed little Bruce, who was still asleep in his chair. He grabbed his bag and shut the door. He walked to the airport then looked back, waving at his wife and son.

Misty pulled off the airport. She was wondering to herself how Elliot was going to react after he read the letters she put in his bag. She had made a copy of her letter for herself, so she gave him the original one. She returned to the apartment, put little Bruce in bed with her, and quickly fell asleep. She stayed in bed, sleeping off and on and waiting for Mya, who was supposed to come over after her duty this afternoon.

At 5:00 p.m., Elliot called to let Misty know that he arrived in Detroit and that he was on his way to the apartment with his teammates.

Mya arrives at the apartment. Mya was sitting on the couch. She asked Misty, "How are you doing, girl? Does he know yet?"

Misty replied, "Hell no." She told Mya that she didn't know how he was going to react.

Mya asked her, "Then when are you going to tell him, Misty?"

Misty told Mya that she had put the letter in his bag in a pocket. She said that he'll find it sooner or later, but he will find it. Mya told her that she probably should have just told him, and it would have cut out a lot of confusion. Misty agreed with her, but she said, "I just couldn't, Mya. I still love him. He's all I know."

Mya said, "I know, Misty. No one can even imagine what you are dealing with right now. I couldn't do it, girl. Let me ask you this, Misty. Tell me you didn't give him any."

Misty said, "Yes. I had to."

Mya replied, "Oh my god! Oh my god!"

Elliot's first professional game was on Sunday at 1:00 p.m. in Minnesota, and Elliot was supposed to be starting as running back.

He actually was the second string back, but the original starting running back was hurt in preseason, so it was all up to Elliot Bennett.

Misty and Bruce were watching the television, and they saw Elliot come out of the tunnel as they called his name as a starter.

The game had started, and Elliot was killing them. He was running over everyone. He was catching the ball as well as blocking. The Lions were still losing the game, but Elliot was proving to be a star running back. At the end of the game, the reporters interviewed him, and right on television, he said "I want to send a shout out to my lovely wife and my little son, Bruce. I love y'all."

Misty's tears started running down her face. She knew that he evidently hadn't seen the letter yet. She knew it was coming.

The next game was at New Orleans. Again, Elliot got to start. They were calling his name every other play. He scored a touchdown, and when the camera got a close up, Elliot said, "Love you, honey." Misty again started crying. She couldn't believe that he hadn't seen the letter yet.

The next game was a home game in Detroit. This time, Misty, Mya, and another friend of theirs were watching the game at a sports bar in Jacksonville. The announcer came on, and they started announcing the starters for the Lions. They started calling the team, but the name they called for the starting running back was another unknown name. Everyone in the bar knew that Misty was married to the football star, Elliot Bennett. So they were cheering until Elliot appeared to be a no-show. The announcer's made a comment that "The Detroit Lions starting running back Elliot Bennett went missing on Friday before the team meeting, and no one has seen him since." The announcers were saying that they would relay any information that they found as it came.

So the game started, and Misty and Mya left the bar to go back to the apartment. Misty hadn't heard from Elliot the whole week. She started to worry now. She regretted the fact of how she relayed the horrible test results to him.

She was now confused as to what to do. She refused to call Steve and Jean because she hated them. Misty just held her cell phone in her hand and close to her heart. She started praying as Mya drove. Mya appeared as though she had tears in her eyes as well.

Elliot was on a plane to Atlanta. He was going to his parents' house. He read the letter that Misty wrote him. It read,

Dear love, I love you from the bottom of my heart, but I can't love you for the simple fact that you are my fraternal twin brother who was thought to be dead. Steve and Jean rescued you from that bus accident, and they kidnapped you and raised you under another name. Your real dad was Bruce, whom you did meet. I think that he knew who you were. You and I share an identical foot-shaped birthmark on our backs, and I saw yours after I found all of these out. I think Daddy saw this, and that's the reason why he reacted the way he did when you bent over at the hospital. We are twins who have been lied to and fooled. Now we have a beautiful 15-month-old son, and I believe that I'm pregnant again. I just don't know what to do, but we can't continue this because now that we know the truth, it's now a sin because it's incest. You are the only man I ever loved, but now I can't do this anymore.

Elliot was crying in the plane as he was reading it. He was so mad. He said to himself, "I could kill Steve and Jean for what they've done."

He landed at the Atlanta airport, and he rented a car to drive to Macon. On the way to his parents' house, he stops in a local gang-infested hood in Atlanta. He stopped a thug and told him that he would pay $2,000 for a loaded piece. The hood immediately gave up his gun and ran across the street to bring him another one. The hood was happy; he thought he'd just hit a jackpot. He recognized Elliot from the football teams.

Elliot made his way to his parents' house unannounced. He pulled up in the driveway, and it was dusk. The butler came to the door, and he alerted Steve that someone was at the door. He said there was a big fella at the door. He had never met Elliot. Steve saw who it was, and he said, "Let him in. That's my son."

Elliot came in, and Steve tried to hug him. Elliot threw him to the ground. Jean comes running out and she immediately gets on the ground to check on her husband.

Elliot started screaming, "Why did you do this to me? Why? You have destroyed me and my family. My son is paying the price for this, and you allowed me to marry Misty and you knew!"

The butler is terrified. Elliot told him to get on the floor. Steve tried to compromise with Elliot. He told him very humbly, "You mother and I were wrong, but when I saw you lying by that bus on the ground, I just wanted to give you the best life possible 'cause I knew that you lost your family. I didn't mean for this to happen, son. We love you, and we wanted the best for you."

Elliot was startled. His tears were really rolling down his face. Elliot called 911. He said, "Come to 37753 Melody Brook Lane 'cause I'm going to kill a few people here."

The police showed up to the house in minutes. There were several police cars. A SWAT team came, and a helicopter was flying around.

Elliot had finally lost his mind. Steve, still pleading with Elliot, said, "Son, please let your mom go 'cause she had nothing to do with this."

Elliot said, "Hell, no! You both have destroyed me and my family. You taught me about honesty, and you have lied to me my whole life. My name is Mitchell, damn it! I hate you, Steve."

While Elliot had them at gun point, he pulled out a piece of paper and started to write his wife a letter. It said,

Honey, I love you, and I never meant for anything like this to happen. You've lost a lot of people in your family. You lost a brother as well. You see, I was really dead to you in your life. Elliot really never existed because Elliot was a lie from the beginning. You need to marry and have a good life because you deserve it. Please take care of Bruce and always tell him that his uncle really loved him. I love you, Misty.

He signed it, "Your brother Mitchell."

The police were outside with the bullhorns, trying to plead with Elliot. He acted as if he didn't hear them. He put the letter in an envelope and gave it to the butler. He told the butler to take it to the police and tell them to give it to his wife. The butler said, "Okay, sir." The butler did as he said.

Elliot pointed the gun at Steve and then he pointed it at Jean. He said, "I can't," then he put the gun in his mouth and pulled the trigger.

Misty had her husband brought home to Valdosta for his funeral. Thousands attended. Steve and Jean were brought up on kidnapping charges. It was a really sad time.

It had been two months since the funeral. Misty and Bruce went to visit the gravesite, and she looked at the tomb, and there were four names on the family plot. There was Leatha, Bruce, Mitchell, and there was Elliot. Although there were only three bodies in the actual grave, the grave held four people.

Misty got Bruce, and they jumped back into the car to go home. Misty had bought a home down the street from the cemetery because she wanted to be close to her family.

THE END

About the Author

Thomas E. Valentine Jr. is a Detroit, Michigan native who attended Detroit Osborn High School and Fort Valley State University in Fort Valley, Georgia. He has resided in Birmingham, Alabama, Memphis, Tennessee, and also Jacksonville, Florida. Thomas served in the United States Navy and fought in the Desert Shield Desert Storm War. He was honorably discharged in 1991. This is Thomas' first published book with many more to come. Thomas loves to write about controversial issues that make you think and wonder. He is happily married to Geisha Mia Valentine. Thomas loves to sing karaoke and loves all types of music. Thomas also enjoys camping, photography, and cruising the Caribbean. Thomas' goals are that his writings will end up in movie production someday.

CPSIA information can be obtained at www.ICGtesting.com
Printed in the USA
BVOW04s1935201015

423359BV00011B/99/P